THE BOOKS OF
eLSeWHeRe
volume three
THE SECOND SPY

THE BOOKS OF
ELSEWHERE
volume three
THE SECOND SPY

by Jacqueline West

illustrated by Poly Bernatene

DIAL BOOKS FOR YOUNG READERS
an imprint of Penguin Group (USA) Inc.

DIAL BOOKS FOR YOUNG READERS
A division of Penguin Young Readers Group
Published by The Penguin Group
Penguin Group (USA) Inc., 375 Hudson Street, New York, NY 10014, U.S.A.
Penguin Group (Canada), 90 Eglinton Avenue East, Suite 700, Toronto, Ontario, Canada M4P
2Y3 (a division of Pearson Penguin Canada Inc.) · Penguin Books Ltd, 80 Strand, London WC2R
0RL, England · Penguin Ireland, 25 St. Stephen's Green, Dublin 2, Ireland (a division of Penguin
Books Ltd) · Penguin Group (Australia), 250 Camberwell Road, Camberwell, Victoria 3124, Aus-
tralia (a division of Pearson Australia Group Pty Ltd) · Penguin Books India Pvt Ltd, 11 Commu-
nity Centre, Panchsheel Park, New Delhi - 110 017, India · Penguin Group (NZ), 67 Apollo Drive,
Rosedale, North Shore 0632, New Zealand (a division of Pearson New Zealand Ltd) · Penguin
Books (South Africa) (Pty) Ltd, 24 Sturdee Avenue, Rosebank, Johannesburg 2196, South Africa ·
Penguin Books Ltd, Registered Offices: 80 Strand, London WC2R 0RL, England

Designed by Jennifer Kelly
Text set in Requiem
Printed in the U.S.A.

1 3 5 7 9 10 8 6 4 2

Library of Congress Cataloging-in-Publication Data
West, Jacqueline, date.
The second spy / by Jacqueline West ; illustrated by Poly Bernatene.
p. cm. — (The books of Elsewhere ; v. 3)
Summary: After plummeting through a hole in her backyard and finding
herself once again in the room of mysterious jars, eleven-year-old Olive
unwittingly releases two of Elsewhere's biggest, most cunning, most
dangerous forces.
ISBN 978-0-8037-3689-4 (hardcover)
[1. Space and time—Fiction. 2. Dwellings—Fiction. 3. Magic—Fiction.]
I. Bernatene, Poly, ill. II. Title.
PZ7.W51776Se 2012
[Fic]—dc23   2011027236

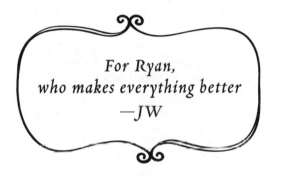

For Ryan,
who makes everything better
—JW

I F YOU BELIEVE that death is about to spring upon you at any moment, you won't spend much time watching television. You won't devote a lot of thought to bathing or tooth-brushing, either. Even things you once enjoyed, like reading, doodling, or daydreaming, will slide right off of your daily to-do list.

If you believe that death is coming for you, you'll do a lot of jumping around corners. You'll turn on all the lights in every room you enter, even on bright August afternoons. You will get surprisingly good at walking backward up staircases. You will never forget—not even for a minute—that doom could be waiting just through any doorway.

Your life will revolve between two things: spending as much time as possible with those you care about, and *hiding*.

Fortunately for Olive Dunwoody, who was whiling away the end of the summer in this particularly uncomfortable situation, she had the perfect way to do both.

Each morning, as soon as her parents were busy with their own work and worries, Olive put on the pair of antique spectacles that hung from a ribbon around her neck. Then she stepped from her bedroom into the hallway of the old stone house on Linden Street and watched the paintings that lined its walls ripple into life.

Painted grass waved in an intangible wind. Painted trees twitched. Painted people moved and blinked and stared back at her from the other side of their canvases.

Grabbing the edges of the picture frame that hung just outside her bedroom door, Olive would squish herself through the wavering, jelly-like surface, fall with a flop into the misty field, and bolt up the painted hill to find her friend Morton.

Morton was nine years old. He had been nine years old for a lot longer than eleven-year-old Olive had been eleven. In fact, he'd been nine years old for longer than Olive had been alive.

An old man's lifetime ago, Morton had lived with his family right next door to the old stone house on Linden Street. No one who lived right next door could have helped but notice something odd about the place . . . and about the McMartin family, who lived in it. Finally, the day had come when Morton's family knew too much.

Aldous McMartin, the painter and patriarch of the McMartin family, got rid of Morton by trapping him inside a painting. Morton's sister, Lucinda Nivens, who had hoped to be accepted into the McMartin family and taught their magical secrets, had eventually been betrayed and killed by the people she served. As for Morton's parents, they had vanished. No one knew where.

Well . . . not *no one.*

Annabelle McMartin knew.

But she wasn't about to tell.

To begin with, Annabelle McMartin was dead. She'd finally croaked at the age of 104, the last twisted twig on the McMartin family tree. Because she had died without an heir, all of the McMartin family treasures were left to clutter the corners and hang from the walls of their old stone house on Linden Street. The inconvenience of being dead should have kept Annabelle and her ancestors from causing anyone any trouble. But that was not the case. Not in *this* case. For among the many odd, dusty relics the McMartins had left behind were their portraits—magical, living, conniving portraits, painted by Aldous and craftily hidden in the house's depths. These portraits wanted nothing more than to take their house, with all its secrets and powers and history, *back.*

Olive had discovered this in the most unpleasant of ways.

The knowledge that the living painting of her home's former owner was on the loose, intent on revenge, was what had Olive jumping around corners and backing up staircases. Sometimes her eyes played tricks on her, and she would catch the flash of a painted tendril of long brown hair in the gleam of a wooden banister, or the sheen of a string of pearls floating above an empty chair. Annabelle's too-sweet, too-still smile seemed to glitter from the shadows of the house's darkened rooms.

This usually happened when Olive was alone.

Olive tried to be alone as little as possible.

When she was with Morton, she felt a bit less frightened. Her fear seemed to spread out between them, like a dose of awful medicine divided into two spoons. Together, Olive and Morton would slip through the creaking, cluttered rooms, climbing in and out of Elsewhere. They searched painting after painting for some sign of Morton's parents. They questioned every painted person they met. They flipped over every painted rock (the rocks always flipped themselves hurriedly upright again), they peered inside painted windows, and they peeped through the keyholes of painted doors. But when every rock had been flipped and every keyhole had been peeped, they still hadn't found a single new clue.

Fortunately, the search mixed some fun into the frustration. Sometimes Olive and Morton visited the painting of a ruined castle, where a painted porter happily led them on tour after tour. They scattered chubby pigeons on a painted Paris sidewalk. They clambered through the frame of a painted ballroom and danced to the music of the out-of-practice orchestra. If the house's kitchen was deserted, they dove into its painting of three stonemasons and played with Baltus, the large, shaggy dog that Olive had rescued from another painting. When they were feeling especially brave, they even went boating on the smooth silver lake where Annabelle had once left Olive to drown.

Often, one of the house's three guardian cats would accompany them. The cats could slip in and out of Elsewhere as easily as they slipped in and out of the house's many rooms. Olive would spot the spark of green eyes in the distance, across the painted waves of a river or between the brush-stroked petals of a blooming garden, and she would feel her fear spread even thinner, knowing that the cats were watching over her.

But nothing could lift the fear away completely.

And as the last days of summer tiptoed past, something else was creeping up on Olive. Something that swelled and darkened like a bruise in the back of her mind. Something even bigger and blacker and chillier than her own untimely and quite-possibly-impending death.

Junior high.

A FAMOUS POET ONCE wrote that April is the cruelest month. Olive knew this because she had come across the poem somewhere in the dusty library of the old stone house on Linden Street. She hadn't understood most of the poem, but she remembered the line about April. She remembered it because it was so obviously untrue. Olive knew—as all kids know—that the cruelest month is September. One morning, you wake up to a sky that still feels like a summer sky, and a breeze that still feels like a summer breeze, and you smile, looking forward to a whole day of freedom—and then your mother shouts up the stairs that you're already running fifteen minutes late, and if you don't get a move on, you'll miss the school bus.

This was just what happened to Olive. Except she didn't wake up looking forward to a day of freedom and adventure. She woke up exhausted, with a cramp in her legs from a night of dreams about a furious witch chasing her around and around a giant hamster wheel. As she squeezed Hershel, her worn brown bear, Olive told herself that these had been nothing but nightmares. The problem was, except for the giant hamster wheel bit, Olive's nightmares might come true.

"Olive!" Mrs. Dunwoody called from the foot of the stairs. "You're now seventeen point five minutes late and counting!"

With a sigh, Olive tucked Hershel back under the covers. She stood up in bed, wavering for a moment on the squishy mattress, and then jumped as far away from the bed as she could get without crashing into another piece of furniture. Olive did this every morning, just in case something with long, grabbing, painted arms was waiting underneath the bed. From several feet away, she bent down to check under the dust ruffle. No Annabelle. Olive opened her closet with a practiced yank-and-leap-backward maneuver. This way, if Annabelle were indeed waiting inside, Olive would be hidden behind the door. She peeped through the door frame. No Annabelle. Olive tugged on a clean shirt, carefully arranging the spectacles inside the collar, and hustled out into the hallway.

Even on clear September mornings, the upstairs hall of the old stone house remained shadowy and dim. Faint rays of sun glinted on the paintings that lined the walls. Olive's fingers gave a twitch. The temptation to put on the spectacles and dive into Elsewhere tugged at her like a strand of hair caught in a rusty zipper.

"Olive!" called Mrs. Dunwoody. "There are just thirty-four minutes until the school day begins!"

With a last longing glance over her shoulder, Olive headed for the stairs, slipped on the top step, and just managed to catch herself on the banister before toppling rump-over-teakettle down the staircase.

Because it was Olive's very first day of junior high school, Mr. Dunwoody had fixed a special pancake breakfast. Mrs. Dunwoody kissed Olive on the head and told her how grown-up she looked. Then Mr. Dunwoody made her pose for a photograph on the front porch holding her book bag and her fancy graphing calculator, and after that, Mrs. Dunwoody drove her to school because she had already missed the bus and if she walked she *would* have been tardy by more than fifteen minutes. And yet neither of her parents noticed that Olive (whose brain was even more distracted than usual) was still wearing her pink penguin pajama bottoms with ruffles across the seat of the pants.

But the kids at school did.

Everyone in Olive's homeroom laughed so loudly that students walking down the hall stopped to see what was so funny. One boy laughed until his face turned the color of kidney beans, and he had to go to the nurse's office to use his asthma inhaler.

A girl with long, dark hair and a sharp nose—a girl who, Olive noticed, was wearing *eyeliner*—leaned across the aisle to Olive's desk. "They're mean, aren't they?" she asked. "Don't worry about them," the girl went on as Olive tried to squeeze out an answer. "I think your pants are *adorable*." Here the girl raised her voice a little bit, so that everyone around them could hear. "But didn't you know that the *kindergarten* is in another building?"

All the kids went off on another roar of laughter, and Olive wished she could sink down into the cracks in the floor with the eraser scrapings and pencil dust.

The morning didn't get any better. During her second class, when the students were supposed to stand up and tell about themselves, Olive mumbled that she was eleven, that her parents were both math professors, that her family had moved to town at the beginning of summer, and—because she couldn't think of anything else to say—that she had a birthmark shaped very much like a pig right above her belly button, which was true, but which she certainly hadn't planned to admit to anyone.

During her third class, Olive asked to go to the restroom and got so lost afterward that she wandered around the building for almost an hour and wound up in a storage room behind the gymnasium, where a friendly janitor finally found her.

When lunchtime came, Olive tiptoed into the cafeteria with a fleet of butterflies doing death-spirals in her stomach. The tables were already crowded with students (Olive had gotten lost on the way to the cafeteria too), and everyone was shouting and laughing and stealing food from one another's trays. She blinked around, wondering how she was ever going to feel brave enough to sit down at one of those tables, and whether it would be dangerously unsanitary for her to take her lunch back to the restroom and eat it there, when, like one stalled car in a sea of roaring traffic, a quiet table surfaced amid the chaos.

The table was empty except for one rumpled boy. A boy with smudgy glasses, and messy brown hair, and a large blue dragon on his shirt.

Large blue dragons had never looked friendlier. Olive made a beeline for the table.

"Hi, Rutherford," she said, smiling for the first time all day.

Rutherford Dewey glanced up. Before Olive had even had time to plop into a chair, he asked, "Have you heard about the pliosaur skull that was discovered on the Jurassic coast?"

There were several questions Olive could have asked in response to this. ("Where's the Jurassic coast?" "What's a plierssaur?" "Is that its name because it looks like a pair of pliers?") But the only answer she could give was "No." So she gave it.

"It's a fascinating find," Olive's neighbor went on, in a rapid, slightly nasal voice that was only partially muffled by a mouthful of chicken salad. "The skull itself is nearly eight feet long. The pliosaur's entire body probably measured around fifty feet, which is more than twice the size of an orca."

"An orca is a killer whale, right?" asked Olive, unwrapping her sandwich.

"Yes, although the name 'killer whale' is a bit unfair. The orca isn't an especially murderous creature. Besides, all of us are killers of *something*."

"No we're—" Olive cut herself off mid-argument, wondering if dissolving something evil that came out of a painting counted as "killing."

Rutherford watched her take the first bite. "What's that in your sandwich?" he asked.

"Peanut butter."

"Then you're a peanut killer. It's inevitable. Each of us has to kill to survive."

Olive squirmed. For the hundredth time that day, she touched the lump of the spectacles underneath her shirt, making sure they were still there.

"Don't worry," said Rutherford. "My grandmother will be keeping a very close watch on the neighborhood while we're at school. She'll be watching your house especially."

Olive glanced up into Rutherford's intent brown eyes. Not for the first time, she had the strange feeling that Rutherford must have been reading her mind. Of course, she reminded herself, it wouldn't be hard for him to *guess* what she was worrying about.

"Your grandmother hasn't seen any sign of . . . of *Annabelle,* has she?" Olive asked, dropping her voice to a whisper.

Rutherford shook his head, looking unconcerned. He looked just as unconcerned a second later, when a wad of plastic wrap sailed through the air and beaned him on the head. "No. No sign of her presence," he went on as a group of boys at a table nearby slapped each other's hands and sniggered. "And my grandmother has also placed a protective charm on your house, which prevents anyone who isn't invited inside from entering the house itself. She uses the same kind of charm on ours. It dates back to the middle ages, when it was placed on the walls of castles and fortresses, and thus it doesn't protect outdoor spaces; however, it is still quite effective." Noticing that Olive's eyes were beginning to glaze, Rutherford changed the subject. "Have you heard about Mrs. Nivens?"

Olive almost inhaled a chunk of sandwich. She looked around, making sure no one else had heard. "What about her?"

"The police have declared her a missing person. They've searched her house and everything. Now it's locked up and they're keeping it under surveillance."

Olive put down her sandwich. "I don't think they'll figure out what really happened. Do you?"

One of Rutherford's eyebrows went up. "You mean, that Mrs. Nivens was actually a magical painting trying to serve a family of dead witches, one of whom finally turned on her?" The eyebrow came down again. "I think it's highly unlikely."

"Yeah." Olive paused. "They sure won't figure it out from looking around her house. Everything is so *normal*." Olive's mind darted back to the evening when she, Morton, and the cats had tiptoed through the eerily clean and quiet rooms of Mrs. Nivens's house— a house that had hidden Mrs. Nivens's secret for nearly a century.

A not-quite-empty carton of milk hit the center

of their table, exploding in a fountain of tepid white droplets. The boys at the nearby table guffawed.

"It's been my experience that those people who seem the most 'normal' are in fact the most dangerous," said Rutherford, wiping a drip of milk off the end of his nose.

Olive dragged her penguin-dotted legs through the rest of the afternoon. She spent science class staring at the shelves of beakers and test tubes, remembering the chamber full of strange, murky jars that she'd found beneath the basement of the old stone house, and missing half of the instructions for the very first assignment. Next, she spent history class thinking about all the people Aldous McMartin had trapped inside his paintings, becoming so absorbed that she didn't hear the teacher calling on her until he'd said her name three times. But the minutes ticked by, and the last hour of the day crawled closer, and finally, Olive found herself climbing the stairs to the third floor and trudging along the hall to the art classroom.

Olive pulled up a metal stool to a high white table as far away from all the other students as she could get. Then she waited.

And waited.

And waited.

"Where do you think the teacher is?" asked one of

the noisy girls at the front of the room, after several minutes had gone by.

"Maybe we should call the office and tell them she's not here," said the noisiest girl of all, craning around on her stool so that Olive caught a glimpse of eyeliner.

But before Olive could give another thought to makeup or meanness or penguin pajamas, there was a sound outside the art room door. It was a jingling, stomping, crinkling sound, as though a reindeer pulling a sleigh made of candy wrappers was trying very hard to get in. A key rattled in the lock. "Darn it," said a muffled voice. The doorknob rattled again. In another moment, the door burst open, revealing a woman standing in the hallway.

Her arms were filled with paper and plastic bags, which in turn were filled with other things—pipe cleaners, canisters of salt, and something that appeared to have once been a massive starfish—and her neck was looped with lanyards and whistles and cords and pens and beads and bunches of keys, all clattering together like an office-supply wind chime. Long, kinky tendrils of dark red hair could be seen above the bags, standing out in every direction. With a grunt, the woman dumped the armload of bags on the front table and blinked around at her wide-eyed students.

"Of course, the door wasn't locked at all," she said, as though they were already in the middle of a conversation. "You all got in here. And *you* don't have keys." She glanced into one of the overstuffed paper bags. "Oh, shoot. I think I cracked my cow's skull." Sighing, the woman turned toward the chalkboard. "My name is Ms. Teedlebaum." She wrote something that looked like "Ms. Tood—" and ended with a squiggle. The noisy girls at the front of the room snorted with giggles.

Ms. Teedlebaum turned back toward the class. "We're going to begin this unit at the beginning," she said, putting her hands on her hips. The lanyards and cords and keys swayed and jangled. "And we'll start with a subject you're all familiar with. Yourselves." She turned one of the paper bags upside down, and a flood of pencils and watercolor palettes and oil pastels and chalk bounced out onto the table. Some of the flood bounced all the way to the floor. "You can use whatever medium you like. There are mirrors in that cabinet, and paper is on that shelf. Get started."

With a swish of her long skirts, Ms. Teedlebaum picked up one of the paper bags and sailed toward her desk. At least, Olive *thought* it was a desk. It looked more like a sandcastle built out of art supplies, but there was probably a desk in it somewhere.

"But what are we supposed to do?" asked the girl with the eyeliner, in a tone that strutted along the line between *not quite polite* and *very rude*.

Ms. Teedlebaum glanced up from behind the sand-castle. "Self-portraits. Didn't I say that? No? Yes. Self-portraits. Draw, paint, or color yourselves. Whatever feels right to you."

With more muttering and giggling, the class jostled each other for the best supplies. Olive waited until everyone else was seated again before slinking across the room. The only things left on the front table were two charcoal pencils and a set of mostly broken chalk. She took the pencils back to her seat. Then she stared down at her own reflection in the little round mirror.

Staring back up at her was a girl with stringy brown-ish hair—a girl with a suspicious lump beneath her shirt that might have been the outline of some very old spectacles. The girl's eyes met Olive's. Her eyes were wide and watchful, and more than a little bit afraid.

OLIVE LET HER heavy book bag thud to the floor of the entryway. The thud echoed away through the old stone house, threading like an unanswered voice through the empty rooms. "I'm home," she called, very softly. The walls seemed to lean in around her. Whether they were welcoming her or watching her, Olive wasn't quite sure.

On the first floor, everything was as it should have been. The paintings hung in their places and the furnishings stood in their usual spots. No one with strangely streaked, shiny skin waited on the dusty velvet couch in the library. No one sat tapping her chilly fingers on the heavy wooden table in the dining room. No one with painted gold-brown eyes whispered Olive's name from a darkened doorway.

Olive finished her survey in the kitchen, where a note in her mother's handwriting hung on the refrigerator door. "We hope you had a wonderful first day at school, dear," it read. "We'll be back between 5:34 and 5:39, depending on the usual variables." Olive scanned the kitchen. There was no sign of Annabelle there, either. In fact, it was hard to imagine Annabelle in a kitchen at all, with her pearls and lace amid the Tupperware and dish soap. But this *had* once been Annabelle's kitchen. She had probably stood in the very spot where Olive was standing now. She'd sat everywhere that Olive sat, bathed in the tub where Olive bathed. The thought sent a swarm of invisible spiders skittering down Olive's arms.

Shaking the spiders away, Olive darted for the basement door. An icy waft of air swirled around her ankles as she yanked it open. She had acclimated to almost all the oddities of the old stone house—the creaks and groans it made at night, the cobwebby corners, the low ceiling edges that seemed designed to bash people on the skull—but she hadn't quite gotten used to the basement. Olive stood in the doorway for a moment, gazing down the rickety wooden stairs into the darkness and pulling her courage tight around her. Then, with a deep breath, she rushed down the steps.

"Leopold?" she called, swatting for the lightbulb chain.

"At your service, miss," said a gravelly voice.

Olive found the light at last, and a dusty glow flooded the basement. It flickered on swathes of hanging cobwebs, drew shadows between the gravestones in the walls, and glinted in a pair of bright green eyes that looked up at Olive from the darkest corner of all.

Leopold sat at attention in his usual station, his sleek black chest puffed up so high that it nearly eclipsed his chin. Olive dropped to her knees in front of the gigantic cat. Between them, the outline of a trapdoor made a deep slash in the floor.

"How was your first day of school, miss?" Leopold asked.

Olive sighed and rubbed her chilly arms. She glanced around at the crumbling stone walls, skimming the carved names of the McMartin ancestors, and suddenly realized that she would rather be in a cold, dark basement built out of ancient gravestones than in a junior high classroom. "I'm glad to be home," she answered.

Leopold gave a nod. "They say there's no place like it."

"No, there isn't," said Olive emphatically. "Did anything happen while I was gone?"

"Negative, miss. Nothing to report."

"And the tunnel . . . ?" Olive asked, nodding toward the trapdoor.

"Silent."

"Good. Thank you, Leopold." Olive stood up, brushing the grit from the seat of her pants and wondering why her behind felt so *ruffly*. The relief of being home at last had shooed the flock of pink penguins right out of her mind. Now they waddled rapidly back. "I'd better go check the rest of the house," she mumbled, scurrying sideways toward the basement steps to keep the ruffly area out of Leopold's sight.

Olive skidded along the hall, zoomed around the newel post, and thundered up the stairs to the second floor. She checked each painting as she ran, but the silvery lake, the moonlit forest, and the painted version of Linden Street looked just as they'd looked a hundred times before.

After changing into a pair of jeans and stuffing the pink penguin pajama bottoms under her bed as far as they would go, Olive searched the upstairs hall. She looked into the empty bathroom, the empty blue bedroom, and the empty lavender bedroom, which felt the emptiest of all. Annabelle's portrait—without Annabelle in it—still hung there, above the chest of drawers. As Olive stared into the deserted frame, she could almost see Annabelle's face surfacing within it, with its cold eyes and tiny, unchanging smile . . . like something long dead rising up from the bottom of a pool of dark water.

Olive ran the rest of the way down the hall.

She rushed past the painting of a bowl of strange fruit, the painting of a church on a high, craggy hill, and—

She stopped abruptly, backing up to stare hard at the hill again.

Olive had never climbed into this particular painting. There were no people to be seen inside of it, and at first glance, there wasn't much else to see either.

But today, the painting had *moved*. Out of the corner of her eye, she had seen the leafy bracken on the hillside ripple with a gust of wind.

Olive studied the painting. It wasn't moving anymore.

In any other house, paintings that moved would have seemed surprising, to say the least. But that wasn't what surprised Olive. It was the fact that the painting had moved when she wasn't wearing the spectacles.

Keeping two watchful eyes on the canvas, Olive placed the spectacles on her nose. Before she'd even lowered her hand again, a flock of birds surged out of the brush on the painted hillside and rose into the sky, their wings flashing, their hundreds of bodies swooping and swirling like a single living thing. Olive let out a delighted little gasp.

This wasn't the first time she had seen things move inside of Elsewhere when she wasn't wearing the spectacles. Morton, Baltus the dog, and the glinting of Annabelle's locket had all revealed themselves to her without the magic glasses. But these were things that had come from the real world and ended up stuck inside Elsewhere. Did this mean that the *wind* in this painting had come from the real world? How had Aldous McMartin managed *that?*

Olive hesitated, feeling curiosity—and the painting itself—tugging her closer. *Come on in!* the canvas seemed to call. *The bracken's fine!*

But there was no time for Elsewhere exploration. Not now. And not *alone.* She still had the rest of the house to check, and two cats to find, and letting down her guard, even for this half minute, was probably a bad idea. Olive turned and swept the hallway with a glance. She was still alone. With a deep breath, she headed onward.

The pink bedroom waited at the end of the hall. Afternoon sun fell through its lace curtains, leaving a pattern of fuzzy golden dots on the floor. The scent of mothballs and old potpourri floated in the air. Olive positioned herself in front of the room's single painting, a picture of an ancient town with an archway guarded by two towering stone soldiers. Even through the spectacles, this painting did not come to life. The painted trees on the distant hills didn't sway as Olive moved closer to the painting, pressing her nose into the canvas until its surface pooled around her face like a wall made of jelly. Olive pushed her head through the painting, and then her shoulders, and then her feet, and all at once, she was on the other side. But she wasn't in an ancient town. She was in a small, dark entryway, where a few slips of daylight outlined the shape of a heavy door.

Even though she had stood in this spot too many times to count, Olive felt a shiver race over her skin as she groped through the darkness for the doorknob. The door swung open with a low groan, and Olive scurried through it, rushing up the dusty stairs into the attic.

The attic of the old stone house looked like an antiques store that had been picked up, shaken hard, and put back down. Old chairs and cabinets and mirrors, some covered by sheets, some covered by cobwebs, were heaped against its angled walls. Stacks of paintings crowded its corners. Sagging boxes and old leather bags and locked steamer trunks towered almost to the ceiling. Rusty tools and bits of china were scattered across the floor, like dangerous confetti. And there, a little bit apart from everything else, stood Aldous McMartin's easel.

A drop cloth covered it now, but Olive knew that the easel held Aldous's final—unfinished—self-portrait. Bending down, she raised one corner of the

cloth, the way you might lift up your shoe after stepping on a particularly large bug, and glanced at the
painting beneath. On the dark canvas, Aldous's bodi-
less hands gave a twitch. One long, bony finger rose,
seeming to point directly at her. With a jerk, Olive let
go of the cloth. She backed hurriedly away from the
easel and collided with an ancient love seat, landing on
her behind with a dusty *whump.*

On the cushions beside her, a splotchily colored cat
bolted upright.

"Zee castle ees undefended!" he cried in a thick
French accent, hurrying to put on his coffee can
helmet by knocking it upside down and cramming his
head into it. "Knights, arm yourselves!"

"It's all right, Harvey—I mean, um . . . Sir Lancelot,"
said Olive. "It's only me."

"Ah," said Harvey. He had gotten the helmet on
sideways, so that only one green eye peeped through
its rectangular slit. "*Bonjour,* my lady," he added tinnily.

"Hello," said Olive, adjusting the coffee can until
both of Harvey's eyes appeared in the eyehole, just
above the words *Bold, Hearty Flavor!* "Did you see anything suspicious today?"

"Zuspeecious?" Harvey repeated. "*Non.* All was
quiet. Zat ees, but for one intruder 'oo attempted to
surmount zee walls of my fortress. 'Ee was defeated."
Harvey nodded proudly toward the floor below, where

a squished spider made an asterisk-shaped blot on the boards.

Olive moved her feet away from the blot. "But no sign of Annabelle?" she asked, watching the spider to make sure it didn't magically regenerate. It didn't.

"I 'ave not zeen her," said Harvey, hopping lightly onto the back of the love seat and promenading back and forth. "She ees likely aware zat zee castle is protected by Lancelot du Lac, zee greatest knight of all!"

"That must be it," said Olive as Harvey lost his footing and slid over the back of the love seat. There was a loud clank from the coffee can.

"Ah-HA!" roared Harvey, leaping back onto the cushions. "Booby traps!? You zink zuch tricks can defeat Lancelot?"

"I've got to see Horatio," said Olive, edging away as Harvey tore into the love seat with all four claws.

Olive hustled out of the attic, back down the upstairs hall, and turned toward her parents' bedroom.

She hardly ever went to this end of the hallway. Her parents' room stood between a small green room that had no paintings in it, and an even smaller white room, which contained only the painting of a cranky-looking bird on a fencepost and dozens of boxes that her parents still hadn't unpacked. After scanning both the green and the white room with the spectacles, Olive opened the door to her parents' bedroom.

It was a large room, and in it was a very large bed. In the center of the bed, a very, *very* large cat appeared to be fast asleep. A beam of sunlight fell through the window directly onto the cat's orange fur, making him glow like some sort of angelic sea anemone. Olive tiptoed closer. Unable to resist, she reached out and ran her hand over the warm, silky ends of glowing fur.

"Hello, Olive," said Horatio, without opening his eyes.

"How did you know it was me?"

"The smell," said Horatio, eyes still closed. "Peanut butter and sour milk."

Olive folded her arms. "You really shouldn't be sleeping on my parents' bed," she said. "You know my mother is allergic to cats."

Horatio stretched, rearranging himself so that the sunlight covered as much of his body as possible. "Yes, that is unfortunate. But sometimes sacrifices must be made to achieve the happiness of others."

"Hmm," said Olive. She watched Horatio's tail, as bushy as a feather duster, flick back and forth over the sun-warmed blankets. "I can't believe you can sleep in the middle of the day when Annabelle is out there somewhere, trying to get back in *here*."

"Perhaps I wanted you to believe I was asleep. Perhaps I wasn't actually sleeping at all." One of Horatio's eyes opened, revealing a slit of sparkling green.

"Annabelle McMartin is not going to charge into this house in broad daylight, Olive, especially not when she knows we're watching for her. She's cleverer than that."

"Then where do you think she is, right now?"

There was a moment of silence. Then Horatio said, "Someplace dark."

An imaginary droplet of cold water ran down the back of Olive's neck. She turned away from Horatio and tried to focus her mind on the two paintings that hung on the bedroom wall. One was of an old wooden sailing ship on a purplish sea. The other was of a white-pillared gazebo standing in a shady garden, half enclosed by towering willow trees. A gangly man in an old-fashioned suit was seated in the gazebo, reading a book. It would be nice to hide in that gazebo with a book of her own, listening to the breeze, smelling the flowers . . . But Olive had more important, more unpleasant, things to do.

"I'm going to check the yard and make sure everything is safe," she said in a brave voice, looking back at Horatio.

"Good," said the cat. His eyes were already closed.

Olive thumped down through the house and out the back door. The garden sprawled before her in all its thorny, leafy chaos. The ancient trees that surrounded the yard seemed to be trying to cover up the mess with a blanket of shadows. Olive walked around the garden's edge. There were no clues hidden among the strange plants, as far as she could tell. There were no footprints in the dirt near the compost pile, or lost pearls on the moss beneath the trees. Olive was beginning to feel sure that she wouldn't find anything interesting at all, when suddenly half of her body plunged straight through the ground.

Her left leg arched behind her in an awkward ballet position, her arms shot out, grasping uselessly at the air, and her chin landed in the grass between a patch of dandelions and an anthill. Gasping for breath, Olive stared at the bustling ants. They ignored her.

By dragging herself on her elbows, Olive managed to pull her lower half out of the ground and to roll, beetle-like, back around. Her heart thumped as she pawed through the grass. Was there an old well out here, overgrown and forgotten? Had some gigantic animal dug its hole in her backyard? Olive looked warily around, but the largest animal she could see was an obese squirrel grooming itself in a nearby maple tree. She leaned over the gap in the grass.

Here, at the farthest edge of the overgrown garden, well hidden by a mat of twigs and leaves, was a hole—a hole so deep that Olive couldn't see its bottom. Its mouth was between two and three feet wide. She ran one cautious hand around its edge. The dirt was bare, so the hole couldn't have been here for long, and its sides were flat, like something cut by a shovel. This hole had been dug by a person . . . and it had been dug recently. Taking a last, sweeping glance at the yard, Olive lowered her head inside and peered down into the darkness far, far below.

OLIVE PREFERRED HER dark places with a little light in them. She was a big fan of light switches and candles and strings of electric Christmas lights, and she wasn't the type to go plunging into a deep, dark cave without a flashlight. So when she fell headfirst through the hole, it was entirely by accident. One moment she was kneeling in the weedy garden, and the next moment, she was making a squealing sound (something like "AaoooOOP!") as she slid down a steep dirt wall into a dark, chilly space far below the ground.

For a moment, all she could do was breathe. Once she was certain that she would go on breathing with or without trying to, Olive took an inventory of her body. Except for her now very dirty shirt, nothing seemed to be damaged, including the spectacles. Shakily, she rearranged herself into a semi-upright position and glanced up at the mouth of the hole, high above.

I've fallen into a trap! said a panicky voice in her brain. *Just like the kind of trap they dig for tigers! Or is it bears?*

No, you're thinking of Winnie-the-Pooh, said another, slightly-less-panicky voice in her brain.

Oh, that's right . . . The Heffalump trap, said the first voice.

Shut up, brain! Olive yelled at herself.

She took a timid look around. The darkness was as dense as chocolate cake, even with the streaks of faint gray daylight trickling in from above. All she could tell for certain was that she was in some sort of enclosed space, deep beneath the backyard. Horatio's words about Annabelle being *someplace dark* trailed unsettlingly through the chaos in her mind.

"Annabelle?" she whispered. Her heart was thundering in her ribs. It made her voice waver. "Are you here?"

There was no answer.

Tentatively, Olive reached out into the darkness until her fingertips met something solid. But what she felt wasn't dirt.

It was stone.

Olive teetered to her feet. As her eyes adjusted to the darkness, the space seemed to widen around her. Soon she could make out solid stone walls, a packed dirt floor, and something to her left that glinted in the wisps of faint gray light. Olive slunk closer. The glint seemed to split and multiply into rows and rows of glints, sparkling back at her. All at once, Olive knew where she was. She was at the end of the tunnel, beneath the basement, in the room full of jars.

Olive had only recently discovered this room for herself, after forcing Leopold to leave his station by using a spell from the McMartins' spellbook. She *still* couldn't understand why the big black cat was so protective of the place. To Olive, it looked like nothing more than a weird storage pantry for things no one would want to eat anyway.

But whoever had dug the hole had known about this place—had known about it, and had managed to get in. And, as far as Olive could tell, there was only one other person who would have been aware of its existence.

Annabelle McMartin.

Olive scanned the room. It wasn't large, and it was clear that she was alone inside of it. She wrapped her chilly arms tight around herself and peered at the crowded shelves. The jars were filled with things she couldn't quite identify: things that were red and powdery, things that were yellow and oily, things that had legs, things that *were* legs, things with petals or thorns or bones. It seemed to Olive that there might have been a few more gaps in the rows than there had been last time she was down here—but there were so many jars, and so many gaps, and so many bits of broken glass scattered across the floor that it was impossible to be sure. And why would anyone want these jars in the first place?

Shivering, Olive turned toward the high wooden table that stood in front of the shelves. Bits of torn paper were strewn across its surface, just as they'd been when Olive first found them a few weeks ago, with their handwritten words all broken apart like the pieces of a raggedy jigsaw puzzle. Olive turned over a few scraps, managing to make out *Gree—* and *—olet* and *mix with b—* by the trickle of distant daylight. A big mortar and pestle covered with orangeish powder stood nearby. Olive reached into the bowl and brought back a fingertip covered with orange dust. She sniffed it. It smelled like a rotten orange peel. Very cautiously, she put out her tongue and tasted it. It didn't taste like a rotten orange peel. It didn't taste like anything Olive had ever tasted before. She wiped her finger on one of the scraps of paper, drawing a little squiggly wave. Then she sighed, chafing her arms, and surveyed the room again.

Clearly, this place was important. Leopold had been guarding it for who-knew-how-long, and now, not one but *two* secret entrances led to it. She had to be missing something. She had missed important things before. And Olive had learned that when she missed something important, it was usually because she was looking at things in the wrong way.

She tugged the spectacles out of her collar and put them on. In the dimness, she stared hard at the rows of jars. Their contents didn't move. No secret words appeared, letter by letter, in their glass walls. She studied the room itself, but everything looked just as it had a moment ago. Olive sighed. She was just about to take the spectacles off again when her eyes landed on the paper on the table.

The little orange squiggle that she'd drawn with her finger was waving and rolling across the page, just like a real wave in a powdery orange ocean.

Sometimes when you put change in a vending machine, there's a long, mysterious pause while the inner workings catch and turn, and the coins slide into the right slot, and you wonder if the drink you ordered is actually going to fall through the swinging door at all. And then, suddenly: *Clank. Thud.* The can of pop appears in the doorway, and it's icy cold, and it's exactly what you wanted. This is what happened in Olive's brain when the little orange wave started to move.

Her feet pounded the packed dirt as she tore along the tunnel, arms out in front of her, barely noticing the near-total darkness. She stubbed her fingers hard against the ladder beneath the basement's trapdoor, but even that didn't slow her down.

"Leopold!" she shouted, flinging open the trapdoor.

The cat sprang off of the moving platform, whirling around mid-flight and landing gracefully on his feet.

"Is that you, miss?" he exclaimed. "But how did you—"

"Leopold, someone dug a hole in the backyard. Down into the tunnel," Olive gasped, hauling herself out of the trapdoor and scurrying across the basement to turn on the light. "I fell through it. Somebody has been in the room down there. With the jars."

Leopold's eyes widened. "Was anything disturbed? Taken? Vandalized?"

"I'm not sure," said Olive. "It looked like there might have been a few less jars on the shelves. But maybe they were just the ones that were already broken."

Leopold paused for a split second, appearing to think. "I'll get the other guardians. We'll examine the backyard."

"I need to put on a clean shirt, but then I'll come outside too," said Olive as Leopold turned away. "Give me just a minute."

Heart pounding, Olive watched Leopold bound up the basement stairs. She waited until the tip of his glossy black tail had disappeared from sight. And then Olive did something so clever and secretive and sly, she herself wondered how she'd come up with it.

She went to the dryer, which stood in one of the basement's cobwebby corners, dug through the clothes inside, and took out the largest T-shirt she could find. She tied the bottom of the shirt in a knot, turning it into a makeshift bag. Then she scrambled back through the trapdoor, down the ladder, and along the tunnel to the stone room. Being careful not to miss a single scrap, she swept all the torn bits of paper from the tabletop into the T-shirt bag. If Annabelle wanted what was in the jars, then she would want what was on these papers too. In fact, if Olive's slowly solidifying theory was correct, the papers might be even *more* important than the jars. She had to keep them safe.

On top of the ragged bits of paper, Olive placed five jars, picking those whose contents had the most widely varied colors. One was powdery and white, another was viscous and black, and the other three were yolk-yellow, deep red, and a beautiful, water-color-ish blue. Making sure not to trip and smash the whole sack, Olive darted back along the tunnel, up the ladder, through the trapdoor, and up the basement steps.

The first floor of the house was quiet. The cats were nowhere to be seen. Scanning every hall and doorway, Olive smuggled the T-shirt up the staircase to her room and stuffed it underneath her bed.

Crouching there, while Hershel, her brown bear, gazed down at her from the pillows, Olive paused to really *think* for the first time. What she had beneath her bed, right next to the pink penguin pajama bottoms and a single dusty slipper, were the ingredients and instructions for Aldous McMartin's magical paints.

An electric shock of joy buzzed through her. A second later, the buzz fizzled into a shiver as she imagined what the cats would do if they found out.

They would take the jars away. They would stop Olive from trying to put the pieces together. They would tell her that dealing with Aldous's magic was wrong and dangerous, and that if she didn't want to become like the McMartins herself, she should simply sweep it out of her mind.

But Olive couldn't do this.

She couldn't let the paints or the papers fall into the wrong hands. And the tunnel clearly wasn't secure, even with the cats guarding it day and night.

Besides, if she figured out how to create them, maybe she could use these paints to do *good*. Maybe she could help the people trapped in the painting of Linden Street. Maybe she could undo some of the evil that Aldous McMartin had left behind. All she needed was time to think. And as long as the cats believed that Annabelle, not Olive, had taken the missing jars and the torn-up papers, then Olive's secret was safe.

Giving the bed one last glance, Olive brushed the dirt off her hands, tugged a clean shirt over her muddy one, and hustled downstairs to join the cats.

Horatio, Leopold, and Harvey had assembled behind the garden shed, out of sight of the house. Their low, arguing voices trailed across the grass toward Olive as she tiptoed closer.

"It's your station," she heard Horatio saying. "Couldn't you keep *one little area* safe?"

"With all due respect," Leopold's gruff voice answered, "the grounds are a shared area. I've examined the hole. It was dug several days ago, possibly weeks. And none of us noticed it. Harvey, didn't you monitor the backyard during night patrol?"

"I am not sure who ees this 'Harvey' . . ." said Harvey's voice, in Sir Lancelot's accent, "but I am neverzeeless certain zat he watched zee backyard with awe-inspiring bravery."

"Indeed," said Leopold. "Then I do not see how—"

"This is *Annabelle!*" Horatio cut him off. Olive crouched behind the shed's open door, listening hard. "Furthermore, it's not the backyard that matters, it's what is *beneath*. Do you both realize what damage she could do with a single one of—"

At just that moment, bumped by Olive's elbow, the shed door gave the kind of loud, rusty creak that makes most people try to use their shoulders to cover their ears. Olive flinched.

Horatio stopped speaking. A second later, the bright green eyes of all three cats appeared around the corner of the shed: Horatio's angry, Leopold's wary, and Harvey's half eclipsed by the coffee can.

"Olive?" said Horatio.

"Oh," said Olive, trying very hard to look casual and fumbling with the shed door so that it gave another violent creak, "so you're not *inside* the shed. I thought you were. Inside, I mean. That's why I—um . . ."

"Well, come over here, so we can speak without shouting to you," snapped Horatio.

Olive scurried around to the other side of the shed and crouched down until she was at cats'-eye level.

"Miss," Leopold began, "we owe you our apologies. I was"—he fought to get the next words out—"an *incompetent* guardian. The security of the tunnel was compromised, and I deserve to be disciplined."

"You desairve to be burned at zee stake!" hissed Harvey, with a knightly toss of his coffee can. "Beheaded! Put on a pike!"

"Hey!" objected Olive, even though it sounded to her more like a reward than a punishment to put a cat on a fish. "You have no right to criticize, considering that I found *you* asleep at your post about half an hour ago."

"Zat is true," said Harvey, in a smaller voice. "But napping ees not treason."

"Annabelle is tricky," said Olive. She looked down at Leopold, who in turn was looking sadly down at his toes. "Almost anybody could be fooled by her."

Horatio let out a long breath through his nose. "She's right," he said at last. "I suppose our only course of action now is to fill in this hole and redouble our efforts."

"The price of safety is eternal vigilance," Leopold mumbled to his front paws.

Olive patted him on the head.

"Leopold," Horatio commanded, "go back inside and patrol the tunnel. Harvey and I will get to work out here. Olive . . ." Olive straightened up, ready to be useful. "Go wash up. Your parents will be home soon, and you look like you've been rolling around in a coal scuttle."

Olive sagged again. She headed toward the back door obediently, wondering what a coal scuttle was. Leopold slumped along beside her. Behind them, Harvey and Horatio were already crouching at the far side of the garden, examining the tunnel's newest entrance.

"You may not see much of me for a while, miss," said Leopold, not meeting her eyes, once the back door was safely shut behind them. "I will be going underground for a time. But if you ever need me, you'll know where to find me." With a nod that lacked its usual soldierly sharpness, Leopold vanished down the basement stairs.

Olive watched him go. Then she stood by herself in the kitchen for so long that her feet began to go numb. She was stacking up a tower of thoughts, and Olive knew that if she moved, the whole tower might come crashing down.

If it *was* Annabelle who had dug her way into the room at the end of the tunnel (and it seemed more than likely that it *was*), then she would almost certainly have taken some of the jars. However, she hadn't taken the papers, which gave Olive a sliver of hope. Furthermore, with or without the paint-making instructions, Annabelle wasn't a painter, as far as Olive knew. It was *Aldous* who was the artist of Elsewhere. What good would the paints be to Annabelle? Olive chewed on a strand of her hair, thinking. What good would the paints be to *her?*

Well, they would be no good at all unless she knew how to concoct them. And in order to even begin to do that, she would have to put together all those thousands of bits of torn-up paper. And that could take *ages,* if she managed to do it without losing her mind first. One Christmas, an aggravating great-uncle Dunwoody had sent Olive a jigsaw puzzle. It was made up of five thousand pieces, and every piece was covered with a broken picture of other puzzle pieces. If you put all five thousand pieces together, you had what looked like another pile of unsolved puzzle bits all tumbled together on a tabletop. Just the idea of putting that puzzle together made Olive's brain start to hiss and sputter like a frying egg.

Even if she *did* manage to reassemble all those torn-up papers, and even if they *were* recipes for paint, and even if she *could* figure out how to use them . . . what would she use them *for*? What could Olive possibly paint that would be worth bringing to life forever?

Olive was still thinking and chewing when the front door creaked open.

"Hello, junior high school student!" called Mr. Dunwoody cheerily as he and Mrs. Dunwoody set down their briefcases. The words *junior high* kicked over Olive's tower of thoughts very efficiently.

Mrs. Dunwoody bustled down the hall, kissed Olive on the head, and went into the kitchen to turn on the oven. "I'll get dinner started, and then we want to hear all about your first day."

And so, from the start of the meal until the end of the evening, the three Dunwoodys talked about school (and about math class in particular), about study habits (about the use of rulers, compasses, and graphing paper in particular), and about the importance of good grades (A-pluses, in particular). By the time Olive climbed the stairs to bed, Mr. and Mrs. Dunwoody were glowing like two delighted jack-o'-lanterns, and Olive was so worn out and worried that she didn't want to do anything but crawl under her blankets, squeeze Hershel, and pile the pillows over her head.

Which was exactly what she did.

SOMETHING SMALL BUT insistent poked at Olive's shoulder. Even through a thick layer of sleep, she could feel it jabbing her arm again and again, as though there were an elevator button on her pajama sleeve. Groggily, Olive shifted beneath the blankets, smooshing her face into Hershel's fuzzy side.

The small, insistent thing kept poking.

"Olive," whispered a voice.

Olive jerked her shoulder away.

The poking shifted to her face. "Olive," the voice whispered again. The small, insistent thing poked her cheek. Poke, poke, poke. *"Olive."*

Olive finally managed to raise her rusty eyelids. She gazed out into the darkened room. From somewhere amid the folds of her blankets, a pair of vivid green eyes stared back at her.

"Good," said a voice with a faint British accent. "You're awake."

"Well, I am now, Harvey," said Olive rather grumpily. "You woke me."

"Shh," whispered the cat. "Someone may be listening. Don't reveal my identity. Call me *Agent 1-800.*"

"What happened to Sir Lancelot?" asked Olive.

"Who?"

"Never mind." Olive closed her eyes again

Harvey's paw gave her cheek another insistent poke. "I have top-secret, high-importance, vital-organ, rush-delivery information," he hissed.

"Vital organ?" Olive repeated.

"It concerns Agent M. Aka *Sir Pillowcase.*"

"You mean *Morton,*" said Olive, eyes still closed.

"Shh!" Harvey hissed again. *"Agent M."*

"What about him?"

Harvey lowered himself toward Olive's face until his nose was nearly touching hers. Olive could feel the wisps of his whiskers against her skin. "Agent M is plotting an escape."

Olive's eyes popped open. "But—he *can't* escape. He can't get out of Elsewhere. Not on his own."

Harvey stalled for a moment, kneading Olive's stomach as he rocked from paw to paw. "Reluctant as I am to inform against a fellow agent," said the cat at last, "I am afraid . . . he tried to bribe me."

"Huh?"

Harvey lowered his voice to a whisper. "He offered to be The Guy That Dies."

"The . . . *who?*" said Olive, wondering if she'd fallen asleep again.

"The Guy That Dies," Harvey repeated. "In any situation we might enact: any duel, any joust, any cannonball volley, I would be the victor, and he would be The Guy That Dies. Meliagaunce to my Lancelot. The Sheriff of Nottingham to my Robin Hood. The good guys to my Captain Blackpaw!"

"Oh."

Harvey tilted his head to one side. "I must admit that I was tempted."

"You didn't say *yes*, did you?"

Harvey stiffened. "Of course not. I am loyal to our cause."

"Then everything's fine."

"I'm afraid not," said Harvey with another poke as Olive tried to close her eyes again. "Agent M is growing desperate. He'll take any opportunity—however dangerous—to get out."

Olive heaved a sigh. "I guess I should go talk to him."

"A wise decision," said Harvey. With an action-hero flip, he leaped off of the bed and slunk toward the door. "Situation comprehensive," Olive heard him mutter into his imaginary transistor wristwatch.

"Sleeper cell has been informed. Now heading to the head of headquarters." A moment later, there came a low creak from the door, and Agent 1-800 was gone.

Olive swung her legs out of bed and jumped to the floor, landing as far away from the bed as she could. She double-checked the hallway for portraits and parents before creeping out of her room, putting on the spectacles, and hauling herself through the frame around the painting of Linden Street.

The moment her feet touched the painting's misty ground, something smacked her in the side with a *thwump*. Olive flailed backward, hitting her head on a corner of the picture frame that dangled in midair behind her and flopping flat on her back in the grass. Something in a white nightshirt landed on top of her.

"MORTON!" Olive choked, once she could manage to breathe again. "What are you *doing*?"

"Tackling you," said Morton, as though this should have been obvious. He rolled off of Olive and glowered at her from the grass. "I aimed for the picture frame, so we'd both fall back out. But you're too *heavy*."

Olive bristled. "Maybe you're too *short*."

Morton jumped up, standing as tall as his three and a half feet would allow. "Maybe you're too STUPID."

Olive took a deep breath and counted to five. On the crest of the misty hill before her, a few lights in the painted houses twinkled faintly.

"Morton," she said, trying to push her voice down into a calm, steady line, "we've already talked about why you have to stay Elsewhere. You're *paint*. People would find out about you, and they'd probably put you in a museum or something. And then they'd learn the truth about this house, and they'd either destroy everything or take it all away to study it, and then we would never find out what happened to your parents."

Morton's round, pale face seemed to soften. Olive was sure he was seeing the logic of her words. Then he said, "You should give me the spectacles."

Olive's hands flew up, grabbing the spectacle frames. "No way!"

"Why should *you* get to have them? *I* could use them. It's *my* parents we're looking for. Besides, you've got the cats. They can take you in and out any time you want. You're just"—Morton stopped, momentarily befuddled—"a spectacle hog."

"I am *not*."

"Spectacle hog! Spectacle hog! Olive is a spectacle hog!" Morton chanted, hopping backward up the misty hill.

"Stop that!" Olive commanded.

"Oink, oink, oink," taunted Morton, before turning and bolting for the street.

Olive chased after him. "Come back here!" she shouted, starting to smile in spite of herself.

Morton's oinks turned to giggles as he led Olive in a looping, zigzagging path up the hill toward Linden Street, his baggy white nightshirt whipping around his legs. Finally, on the edge of a neighbor's foggy lawn, Olive caught him by the elbow, and they both sprawled face-first into the dewy grass, sending up a puff of mist that hovered above them like an impatient cloud.

Olive sat up, laughing. She began to brush the grass off of her pajamas, but each blade had already flown back to its place on the ground, mending and straightening itself. A moment later, Morton sat up too, still giggling. "Oink, oink," he managed, between laughs.

Gradually, Morton's chuckles faded. Olive's panting quieted. Soon the silence of Linden Street surrounded them again, as thick as the mist in the painted air.

The dark houses of a hundred years ago stood before them and behind them, quietly waiting. With their deserted porches and motionless curtains, their quiet rooms and closed doors, they had the air of houses where every inhabitant is fast asleep. Most of the houses were empty, as Olive knew. But here and there, other painted people—others who had been trapped, like Morton—waited inside those curtained windows, staring out into the street even now, watching Olive and Morton, the only things that moved. Nothing else ever changed here. It would be dusk on this misty spring evening for decades—maybe centuries—to come.

"Today was my very first day of junior high," said Olive, after a few quiet minutes had slipped by. "I don't think it could have been any worse if I had accidentally lit the building on fire. Actually, that would have made it better. Because then at least we'd have been sent home early." Olive watched a wisp of mist settle back into place when she shifted her foot. "The kids were mean, the classes were hard, and I wore pajama pants by mistake. And then, when I got home, I found out that somebody had tried to get into the house to steal things. *Again.* Oh, yeah—and an angry witch who can't really die is after me, and she's already tried to drown me and light me on fire, so she's probably coming up with something even worse to do to me the next time she gets the chance."

Morton's tufty head turned away. "I wish I got to go to school," he said.

Olive looked down at the curve of Morton's skinny back. A lump of sadness slid down through her rib cage, coming to rest right on top of her heart. "I'm looking for a way to help you, Morton," she said. "And I *am* going to find your parents. I promised."

"I'm tired of waiting," said Morton into his folded arms. "I've been waiting and waiting, and nothing's happened."

"That's not true," Olive protested. "We found your sister."

Morton's wide blue eyes swiveled back toward Olive's. She could practically read the words *And look how well* that *turned out* printed across his pupils.

Morton turned away again. When he spoke, he appeared to be addressing his knees, which formed two small white hills underneath his nightshirt. "I know you think it's a bad idea," he said. "And I know you won't ever let me have the spectacles. But I'm going to find another way to get out of here. You can't stop me."

Olive tugged on the ribbon that tied the spectacles around her neck, making sure that the knots were tight. "What if we made a deal," she said slowly. "What if you promised not to try to run away, or to trick the cats, or to sneak out of Elsewhere, for the next . . ." Olive paused, counting ". . . four months. If I don't find your parents before that, then you can use the spectacles. For a while. But you have to give them back."

Morton squinted, tilting his tufty head to one side. "*Two* months," he said.

Olive huffed an indignant breath through her nose. "*Three*."

"Deal." Morton put out his hand. Olive took it, feeling surprised yet again by the strange, slick warmth of his not-quite-real skin. Then she slumped forward, leaning her head against her knees. "Just what I need," she muttered. "More pressure. On top of sixth grade, and this house, and Annabelle, now I have a *deadline*."

"I wish I had something extra to worry about," said Morton. He flopped down on his back. "I just want to do something *different*. Everything here stays the same." He pulled up a blade of grass and lowered it gently back toward the ground, watching its roots wriggle gratefully into place.

Something different. The words took hold in Olive's mind like the roots of the painted grass. Morton needed something *different*. Something that would absorb him, and challenge him, and make him feel necessary. He needed a whole obstacle course, or a neighborhood-sized scavenger hunt, or some gigantic five-thousand-piece jigsaw puzzle—

Olive jumped to her feet. "Be right back!" she shouted, already racing down the hill.

Moments later, she was in her own bedroom, rooting among the dust bunnies under the bed. Her hand touched something soft and ruffly, and then something crumbly and dry (which explained where the graham crackers she'd been eating in bed last week had gone), and then something that felt like cotton but was hard and round inside.

With the T-shirt full of torn papers and several rolls of tape from her art supply drawer, Olive slipped back into the hall. Moonbeams from the windows split her shadow into pieces that clustered around her feet like petals around a stem. For an instant, Olive would have sworn that she wasn't alone . . . that someone *else* was tangled in the darkness of that silent hallway.

She stopped, one hand on the picture frame. Her eyes flickered over the nearby paintings: The forest, the silvery lake, the tiny church on its craggy hill. Nothing moved. There was no sound. But Olive got the feeling that the shield around her new secret was already wearing thin. She had to work fast. It wouldn't be long before someone—whether it was a friend or an enemy—found the way in.

THREE MONTHS. *THREE months*. THREE MONTHS to find Morton's parents, or lose Morton himself.

This thought rubbed like a blister against Olive's other thoughts as she struggled through the second day of junior high. She managed to arrive at school in *actual pants* this time, which was a considerable improvement. However, the pants had a mysterious pinkish blotch on the seat, which might have been caused by a laundry mishap, a unique form of mold, or the puddle of Sugar Puffy Kitten Bits that Olive had sat on after accidentally spilling cereal all over the breakfast table that morning. Olive was pleasantly unaware of the blotch's presence until math class, when she was called up to the board to solve a problem and the class erupted into sniggers behind her.

She did the math wrong too.

By the time the last hour of the day arrived, Olive barely had the energy to climb the worn stone stairs to the art room and pull out her stool at the table all the way at the back.

Once again, the art teacher was nowhere to be seen. The students sat at their tables, chattering and squirming and complaining. But as the bell rang and the minutes ticked by, a sense of not-right-ness settled gradually over the room. Stools stopped squeaking. Fingers stopped fidgeting. Students glanced at each other in puzzled silence. Soon the class had gotten so quiet that a soft whistling sound from the back of the room seemed to echo through the air.

Looking for the source of the sound, the other students turned around and stared directly at Olive. Olive, feeling twenty-five pairs of eyes on her, turned around as well. There was nothing behind her but a high white wall. She stared at the wall for a while, pretending that it was the most fascinating thing she'd seen all day. And, as she stared at the wall, something red and curly caught the corner of her eye. Olive glanced down. There, on the floor, with her kinks of dark red hair spread out against the tiles, lay Ms. Teedlebaum. The whistling sound was coming from her nose.

"Ms. Teedlebaum?" whispered Olive. "Are you awake?"

"Unfortunately, yes," said Ms. Teedlebaum. "Would you help me up, please?" Eyes still shut, Ms. Teedlebaum reached out two arms that were covered in clanking rows of bangle bracelets. Olive took Ms. Teedlebaum's hands. The other students watched as the art teacher hefted herself back onto her feet, almost yanking Olive off of hers in the process. Then Ms. Teedlebaum shuffled toward the front of the classroom, pressing both hands to the small of her back and hunching over so that the cords and whistles and lanyards around her neck had an extra-wide range in which to swing.

"I have an old back injury that's acting up today. Circus stuff," said Ms. Teedlebaum, as though this required no further explanation. "You won't mind if I teach lying down today, will you?"

No one answered.

"Good," said Ms. Teedlebaum. With a heavy sigh, she lay down flat on her back on the large table at the front of the art room, turning her face toward the ceiling and closing her eyes.

"We are going to continue our study of portraits for the next two weeks," said Ms. Teedlebaum to the ceiling. "Today, you'll work on your self-portraits. I've labeled your shelves in the cabinet, so you can find your pictures. You know where the other materials are." Here several students gave each other confused looks, but Ms. Teedlebaum, with her eyes closed, didn't notice. "Your assignment for tomorrow is to bring in a photograph. It can be of one person or a group of people, but it has to be *people*. No dogs or cats or unicorns or what-have-you. You're going to work from the photograph to paint the portrait, so make sure it's a nice clear picture. Any questions?" Ms. Teedlebaum asked this without opening her eyes, so it was a good thing that no one raised a hand. "Okay. Get to work."

Ms. Teedlebaum lay motionless on the front table while the students dug through the cabinets to find their unfinished portraits and art materials. It was hard to tell if Ms. Teedlebaum was, in fact, still awake, but by some unspoken agreement everyone tiptoed and whispered, just in case. Olive slipped down from her stool once all the other students were out of the way and brought her self-portrait back to her desk.

She gave the picture a long look. It was both better and worse than she remembered. The shape of her face wasn't too lumpy or off-balance, although her nose looked as though it began in the center of her forehead, and her eyes were either too far apart or too close together—it was hard to tell which. Maybe this was because the eyes were so large overall. Olive picked up her eraser and started rubbing.

While she smudged away the upper end of the nose, she thought about the homework assignment. What picture should she bring in? Mr. and Mrs. Dunwoody were the picture-takers in the Dunwoody house, so most of the pictures in the family albums were of Olive. In fact, if you flipped quickly through the pages of each album, you could watch Olive gradually shrinking or swelling, depending on which direction you flipped.

There were some pictures of Mr. and Mrs. Dunwoody by themselves, taken before Olive had been born—like the one that sat on Mr. Dunwoody's desk, where Alec and Alice beamed at each other in the center of a dance floor, with romantic lights glinting off the thick lenses of their glasses. Neither of her parents was facing the camera, and the glints on their glasses would be tricky to capture.

Olive chewed the inside of her cheek, thinking. What she really needed was a traditional family photo, the kind that people posed for in photographers' studios, where everyone is smiling and looking slightly to the right. She had *seen* a photograph just like this, not long ago . . .

Inside Olive's mind, a flurry of snowflakes began to glitter and spin like the tiny white shards in a snow globe. When they came to rest at last, Olive could see that they weren't snowflakes at all, but fragments of paper—fragments that had arranged themselves to spell out something new. Something *wonderful*. Something that meant she might need a lot less than three months to get Morton's parents back.

For the rest of art class, both Ms. Teedlebaum and Olive remained motionless, one with her eyes shut, one staring straight ahead, neither one seeing anything at all.

The final bell jolted Olive out of her daydreams. Ms. Teedlebaum, on the other hand, didn't even seem to hear it. The art teacher stayed flat on her back on the table as the students put their materials away on the shelves, picked up their book bags, and dashed out the door. Olive waited until the other kids were gone before wandering toward the cabinets. She looked along the shelves for her place, the spot labeled with a little strip of tape that read *Olive Dunwoody*. But as she slid her portrait onto the shelf, she heard the rustle of a sheet of paper. There was something *else* in Olive's spot.

Olive pulled the paper down from the cabinet shelf. It felt thick and brittle at the same time, with soft, battered edges and yellowed corners. On the paper was a portrait, done skillfully in fine black pencil. It was the portrait of a young woman. A young woman with delicate features, long-lashed eyes, and a tiny, chilly mouth. A woman with thick, dark hair—and, nearly out of sight, at the very bottom of the paper, a glistening string of pearls.

The world around Olive became a blur. Her ears filled with a muted roaring sound, as though she'd been underwater in a deep black lake for too long. She couldn't even hear Ms. Teedlebaum sighing behind her, or the table creaking as the art teacher stood up and shuffled toward her desk. The paper trembled in Olive's hands.

"Um . . . Ms. Teedlebaum . . . ?" she croaked.

A jingling sound drifted through the watery roar. "Olive," said Ms. Teedlebaum, leaning over Olive's shoulder, "did you draw that?"

"No," whispered Olive. "I just found it on my shelf. I didn't—I didn't—"

62

"Well, it's very good." Ms. Teedlebaum craned closer. A knot of keys and pens smacked Olive in the back of the head. "Of course, if it *were* your self-portrait, it wouldn't be very good, because it looks nothing like you. But on its own—that's the work of an artist."

"Mm-hmm," said Olive weakly.

"You said you found it on your shelf?" asked Ms. Teedlebaum. "Should I pass it around the classroom tomorrow and see who it belongs to?"

Olive jolted out of her blur. "NO," she said. She turned to face Ms. Teedlebaum, clutching the paper against her chest. "I mean . . . it's *mine*. I just didn't draw it. But it belongs to me." She swallowed. "It came from my house."

Ms. Teedlebaum's eyes had already glazed over. "I forgot to tell the first class to bring bicycle tires tomorrow," she sighed, gazing over Olive's head. "Shoot." With another sigh, the art teacher headed back toward her desk.

"Um—Ms. Teedlebaum?" Olive asked, trying to squish the shakiness out of her voice. "Do you . . . do you know if anyone else has been in here? In this room?"

Ms. Teedlebaum glanced up from behind a mound of clutter on her desk. The kinks of her hair bounced. "In here?" She looked around the room blankly.

". . . Besides the other students, I mean."

"Oh, yes!" Ms. Teedlebaum smiled. "The other students. Yes."

"But has there been anyone *else*? Like . . . could any other *grown-ups* get in here?"

"Well, the janitor comes in every evening, but he doesn't stay long," said Ms. Teedlebaum, rearranging the mound of clutter into a few smaller cluttery mounds. "He really just sweeps the floor these days. He says he's afraid of putting something that might actually be art in the trash again. Hey!" Ms. Teedlebaum crowed. "I've got three bicycle tires right here!"

As Ms. Teedlebaum happily unearthed the bicycle tires, Olive looked back down at the paper in her hands. Annabelle's lifeless eyes gazed up at her. Even in black and white, their stare made Olive's skin break out in goose bumps. To escape their gaze, Olive flipped the paper over—and saw, with a horrible, prickling chill, that something was written on the back.

Oh, Olive, read the paper, in fine, ladylike cursive,

I can't tell you how dull it has been, watching you bumble through the end of the summer, trespassing on our family's property, while I was forced to remain outside. But I knew you couldn't stay indoors forever. I may not be able to get inside your house—my house, that is—but I can reach you anywhere else, at any time I choose. Remember that.

Yes, I've been watching you. And I know what you are about to attempt. Here is my only advice: Do not waste this opportunity, Olive. You don't have much time left, and you may never get this chance again.

Of course, I don't expect you to heed my words. It's hard to know whom to trust, isn't it? Should you do what I say, or the opposite? Can you trust your own closest friends? I believed that I could trust Lucinda—it was she who kept Grandfather's sketch of me safe inside of her house for all these years—and yet in the end she proved to be unworthy. Take a careful look at those you trust, Olive. Because your own friend is hiding a rather large secret from you.

Good luck, Olive Dunwoody.

—Annabelle

"FASCINATING," WHISPERED RUTHERFORD.

Olive and Rutherford were huddled deep in a green vinyl seat, on the bus ride home from school. Annabelle's portrait, note-side up, was tilted against their knees.

"I don't think I'd use the word *fascinating*," Olive whispered back, rubbing her still goose-bumpy arms. "I might use the word *terrifying*."

Behind their smudgy lenses, Rutherford's brown eyes widened. "But she appears to be trying to intimidate you. Don't you know what that means?" He hurried on without waiting for an answer—which was good, because Olive didn't have one. "It means she knows that her real power over you has weakened. She may be trying to trick you into acting irrationally, because she can't *force* you do to anything anymore."

"I don't know," said Olive. "It might just mean she's a witch."

They both studied Annabelle's delicate cursive again.

"And it means she's been watching me, just waiting for me to come out of the house," said Olive, her voice getting shakier no matter how hard she tried to straighten it. "She's been following me. She's been *inside* our school. She could be *anywhere*."

Both Rutherford and Olive craned over the edge of the seat. Two dozen other kids bumped up and down on the green vinyl benches behind them.

"I don't think she's here," Rutherford whispered, lowering himself in the seat again. "Besides, I don't think she's going to pop up in some crowded place and yell 'Boo!' She's just trying to frighten you by revealing that she's been stalking you all along."

"It's working," said Olive. With the very tip of her finger, she underlined part of the note. "Do you think she's telling the truth about—" Olive stopped herself before her secrets could tumble out. It might be nice not to have to make her plans all alone—but it would certainly be safer to keep the secrets locked inside. "About this thing I might be trying to do?" she finished.

"What *are* you trying to do?"

"I can't talk about it yet. I haven't even decided if I'm going to do it in the first place," she said, not meeting Rutherford's eyes, which were boring into the corners of hers like two drill bits. "Do you think she's trying to use . . . what do they call it . . . inverse psychiatry?"

"Reverse psychology?"

"Right. Maybe she knows that if she tells me not to do something, then I'll go do the opposite."

"But she probably knows *that* about you too," Rutherford pointed out.

"So if she knows that I know I should do the opposite of what she says I know . . . ." Olive's head spun. "I don't know."

"It would certainly be a lot easier to discuss this issue if you would just tell me what you might be trying to do," said Rutherford reasonably.

Olive glanced into Rutherford's eyes and turned quickly back to the yellowing paper. "What do you think this part means—that my own friend is 'hiding a rather large secret from me'? Do you think she's talking about one of the cats? Or Morton?" Olive paused to think. "But Harvey just told me Morton's secret: That he was trying to escape from Elsewhere on his own."

"That would be troublesome, to say the least."

"But how would Annabelle know about that?" Olive held on tight to the portrait as the bus hit a bump and everyone bounced up and down. "Who else could she mean? Do you think she meant *you*?"

There was no answer. Rutherford squirmed in the

green vinyl seat. He took off his glasses, huffed on the lenses, and began polishing them on the edge of his red dragon T-shirt. Without the glasses in place, Rutherford's familiar face looked suddenly quite *unfamiliar*. For a long, uncomfortable moment, Olive had the sense that she was sharing a seat with a stranger.

"Does she?" Olive pushed.

"Well—I wasn't going to mention this," said Rutherford, talking even faster than usual, "because until all the arrangements were complete, it just didn't make sense to bring it up, and I'm not sure how Annabelle knew about it, unless she's been spying on me and my grandmother too, which she may very well have been—but my parents have found an international school in Stockholm that has an opening for this fall, and apparently the school's programs are excellent; they teach six different languages, and there are field studies in archeology and paleontology and botany, and of course, it being in Europe, it's in closer proximity to many of the more interesting relics of the Middle Ages, and as you know, I'm an expert in the Middle Ages— though I would naturally prefer that the school was located in Germany or France, where my primary interests lie"—Rutherford went on, polishing his glasses with increasing speed—"however, my parents have promised that we might be able to make some exploratory trips to various Germanic castles during school breaks, of which there are several, even though the academic programs are considered to be extremely challenging . . ."

By the end of this speech, Rutherford was talking so fast that all Olive heard was *veryusgermanicassles-duringskoolbreaksofwitchtherearese veraleeventhotheacademic-programsareconsideredtobeckstreamlychallenging* . . . But this didn't really matter. She knew exactly what he was saying.

"Wait," she cut in. "You mean . . . you're leaving." This was meant to be a question, but there was no question in Olive's voice. "You're switching to another school? In *Sweden?*"

"As I said, the arrangements aren't completed yet," said Rutherford, putting his glasses back on at last. Olive had never seen their lenses look so clean. "But it is highly likely."

For the second time that afternoon, Olive felt the world turn into a blur around her. The bus's metal walls and green vinyl benches suddenly seemed as insubstantial as clouds. She wasn't even sure how her seat was managing to hold her up.

"But—you said—you said you'd be staying here with your grandma for at least a year," she stammered.

"I thought I would be. But then my parents heard about this school and—"

"When would you go?" Olive interrupted.

"I'm not sure; there are still plane tickets to buy and paperwork to fill out, but it makes more sense to transfer at the beginning of the semester than later in the year, when I would have to catch up substantially in every class." Rutherford swallowed audibly. "In other words . . . soon."

"Soon," Olive repeated. There was so much anger in her voice that she felt almost scared of herself. "So you're going to leave. And I'll be alone."

Rutherford looked out the window for a moment before answering. Then he said softly, "You've been alone before."

Olive wasn't sure if it was Rutherford's words or the truth in them, but the statement stung like a slap. She hopped up from the bus seat, grabbing her book bag and the sketch of Annabelle.

"Olive . . ." said Rutherford. But Olive was already charging away up the aisle.

The bus ground to a stop at the foot of Linden Street. Olive leaped down as soon as the doors whooshed open, stalking up the sidewalk as though she couldn't even hear Rutherford hurrying along just a few paces behind her. She and Rutherford were the only kids who got on and off the bus at this corner. As far as Olive knew, they were the only kids who lived on the whole street. With or without the two of them, the average age of Linden Street's residents appeared to hover near the triple digits. Through the changing leaves that hung above her, like a whispering, moth-eaten canopy, Olive could glimpse the angled rooftop of the old stone house. Its dark bulk loomed at the crest of the hill, a piece of midnight thrust into the middle of the afternoon. Olive stormed toward it.

Two doors down the slope from the old stone house, Mrs. Dewey was working in her front garden. At first glance, Mrs. Dewey seemed like an ordinary older lady. She looked as though she had been built out of three large snowballs coated in pink powder and propped on a pair of tiny feet. She raised flowering plants and baked cookies and scolded her grandson for not combing his hair. But with another, more careful glance, a person might notice that Mrs. Dewey was *not* a garden-variety grandmother. In fact, Mrs. Dewey knew quite a bit about the history of Olive's house . . . and about magic itself. She had once saved Olive's life with a charm that included a macaroon and a painted knight figurine. Now, as Olive stomped up the hill, Mrs. Dewey's snowman-shaped figure teetered to its feet.

"Olive!" Mrs. Dewey called out. "Would you like to come inside for some cookies and milk with Rutherford?"

"No thank you, Mrs. Dewey," said Olive, stomping even faster. "I have to get home."

The smile on Mrs. Dewey's face folded into a look of concern as her grandson slumped closer. "I take it you told her," she whispered to Rutherford.

"I told her *something*," Rutherford whispered back.

Then the two Deweys stood together at the edge of their yard, staring after Olive's retreating form.

Olive pounded up the porch of the old stone house and slammed the heavy front door behind her. She threw her backpack onto the floor with such force that it skidded across the floorboards, knocking over an antique coatrack. She leaned back against the door, fuming.

Rutherford was going to leave her. For the first time, she'd had a friend at a brand-new school, and he was going to abandon her. This was even worse than starting from scratch. Now, where only a blank sea of strangers would have been, there would be a hole—a great big gap where something important used to be, and she would have to dodge around it, day after day, trying not to fall in.

Olive kicked the door with her heel. The noise thundered away through the empty house.

She stomped along the hall into the kitchen, yanking the wastebasket from its place under the sink.

Stupid Rutherford. That traitor, she thought, ripping the sketch of Annabelle into smaller pieces with each angry thought. The pieces fluttered down into the wastebasket's mess of coffee grounds and soggy napkins. *Sneaky—Untrustworthy—Secretive—TRAITOR.*

For good measure, Olive grabbed the bottles of ketchup and mustard from the refrigerator and squirted them generously over the shreds of Annabelle's face. Then she stuffed the wastebasket back into its spot.

She didn't need Rutherford. She had other friends— friends that *wouldn't* leave her. She still had the cats. She still had Morton. For now.

Olive swallowed. Annabelle had been telling the truth about more than one thing, apparently: Olive had no more time to waste.

WHEN OLIVE CLIMBED through the frame and into the painting of Linden Street that afternoon, she knew immediately that something wasn't quite right.

The rest of the house was as it should have been. The empty, dusty rooms greeted her one after another, like the pages of a book she'd read a hundred times. Through an upstairs window, she'd spotted Agent 1-800 watching over the backyard from the branches of a towering maple tree, with his fur painted yellow to match the changing leaves, and this had made her feel a smidgeon safer. But here, in Morton's world, something had changed.

At first, she couldn't figure out what it was. Everything *looked* the same. All the houses were where they should have been, every tree and shrub stood in its place, every fallen leaf and acorn sat in its assigned spot. And yet, something strange hung in the air, even thicker than the mist, which in some places was as thick as marshmallow fluff.

Olive trotted warily up the street. Empty lawn after empty lawn greeted her. The houses loomed, sleepy and silent as ever. But from somewhere in the distance came the trace of an unfamiliar sound.

Frowning, Olive trotted a bit faster.

As she reached the crest of the hill, the sound grew clearer, louder, more real, until at last Olive could tell what it was.

It was the sound of voices. A lot of voices. More voices than Olive had ever heard speaking all at once in the muffled world of Linden Street.

Olive sped from a trot to a gallop. The sound of voices grew louder until she reached the edge of Morton's lawn. There she stopped in her tracks.

The porch of Morton's tall gray house was absolutely packed with people. All of his neighbors—the woman in the lacy nightgown, the man in striped pajamas, the old man with the beard, the young woman Olive had only glimpsed in an upstairs window—were sprawled on the floorboards or kneeling in clusters, talking softly, their night-capped heads nodding. A few pairs of slipper-covered feet stuck out between the porch railings. If you threw in pillows and sleep-ing bags and some bowls of popcorn, it would have looked like Morton was throwing a very sedate slum-ber party.

"Olive!" Morton's head popped up amid the crowd. "Come look at what we did!"

Following Morton's impatiently beckoning hand, Olive wound her way up the steps and across the porch, smiling and murmuring hello and trying not to step on anyone.

Morton darted through the crowd and grabbed her by the arm. "Look!" he said in a whisper that was nearly boiling over with excitement. "Look! Look! LOOK!" He pointed toward the center of the porch.

The heap of ragged paper bits that Olive had smug-gled from the basement had dwindled to a handful, like the crumbs left behind by an especially delicious cake. Encircling the remains of the pile, Morton's neighbors huddled over their work, dreamily passing rolls of tape back and forth.

In front of each neighbor lay a reconstructed sheet of paper. The papers were wrinkled and bumpy and almost entirely coated with tape, but they were *there*. Words written in a jagged hand slashed across the pages, dark and whole and clear, even in the faint twi-light. Olive felt as though she was seeing the end of a very difficult magic trick without getting to watch all the wand-tapping and hand-waving that comes in the middle.

She skimmed the top of the nearest page. *Crimson*, it read, in thorny cursive. The headings *Ocher*, *Umber*, and *Emerald Green* seemed to call out to her from other nearby pages.

"Wow," breathed Olive as a mixture of excitement and dread and *rightness* fizzled through her. "I thought so." She looked down at the top of Morton's tufty head. "You know what these are, Morton? These are the instructions for making Aldous McMartin's magical paints."

Morton twitched a little at the name Aldous McMartin. Then he straightened his shoulders. "I already figured that out," he said. "I know what *crimson* means."

"I can't believe you did this so quickly," said Olive.

Morton nodded proudly. "Mr. Fitzroy asked what I was doing, and I let him help," he said, pointing at the bearded man. "Just to make it go faster. Not because I *needed* help. He brought somebody else, and then *she* brought somebody else, and pretty soon everybody was here. And now we're almost done. But I did the most," he added in a whisper.

"Thank you, everybody," said Olive. A dozen pairs of painted eyes gazed up at her. Suddenly, Olive felt a tremor wind its way into her words. "It's—it's so nice of you to help us."

"It's good to have something to do," said the woman with white hair. Her face looked a bit vague, the features soft and unclear. Olive couldn't tell if it was the dim light, or the mist, or if Aldous had somehow made her that way.

"My brothers and sisters and I used to play with jigsaw puzzles when we were children," said the woman in the lacy nightgown. "It helped to pass the time, especially on long winter evenings, when we couldn't go outside, and it seemed like spring would never come . . ." The woman trailed off, looking down at her hands.

"Just what are you planning to do with these papers, young lady?" asked the bearded man who Morton had called Mr. Fitzroy, giving Olive a sharp look.

Olive glanced around the circle of painted faces. "I'm just—I'll—I'm going to keep them safe," she said. "Because I'm sure Annabelle McMartin would love to get her hands on them. I think she already tried to get them once, but maybe she didn't realize how important they were. I mean, *I* didn't know for sure what they were . . . until . . ." Olive looked down at the paper by Morton's feet. *Crimson. Two spoonfuls of dried and powdered blood . . .* Olive swallowed. "But I'm going to make sure she never gets them," she continued, trying to sound firm and confident. "And I'm doing everything I can to make sure she can't use the paints."

"Then wouldn't the safest thing be to destroy them

for good?" said the old man. "Burn them up, so they can't be put back together again?"

Panic shot through Olive's body. "No!" she shouted. The painted people stared at her, their faces unchanging. "I—I just don't think we should do that. Not yet," she hurried on, crouching down to gather the pages into a haphazard pile. "I might be able to learn something from them—like how to help all of you." She clutched the pages to her chest.

The man in the striped pajamas frowned. "Just don't let those *cats* get at them," he said with a warning nod.

"The cats aren't what you think they are," said Olive. "They're good."

"Are you trying to tell us that they *aren't* witches' familiars?" said a bald man with ears that stuck out from either side of his head like the handles on a trophy.

"No . . ." said Olive. "They are. Or they *were*, anyway. But they don't want to work for the McMartins anymore, or to hurt anybody, ever again. The cats are probably the ones who tore up these papers in the first place."

The neighbors were quiet for a moment. Morton stood among them, watching Olive and wavering slowly from foot to foot.

"I wouldn't be so sure about them," said Mr. Fitzroy, breaking the silence at last. "Back in my day, their loyalty seemed to run pretty deep."

"They've changed," Olive argued. "Really."

The woman in the lacy nightgown looked down at her hands. "I suppose they can't hurt *us* anymore, either way," she said.

Everyone was quiet once again. Olive grasped the papers, squirming under the neighbors' stares as the silence seemed to grow even deeper. Whenever she wasn't inside of it, the quiet of Morton's world seemed impossible. There were no rumbling furnaces, no buzzing refrigerators, no distant cars. There were no birds chirping, no breezes whispering. Even amid this crowd of people, there wasn't a single rustle or sigh. Of course, Olive remembered with a little shiver, this was because she was the only one who was breathing.

Olive sidled toward the porch stairs. "Um . . ." she began. "I've got to go. But thanks again for your help. I'll be careful with these, I promise." She halted at the top step. "Oh, Morton," she added, making her voice as light and careless as she could. "I just remembered. Could I borrow that photograph of your family? The one we found in Annabelle's empty portrait?"

Morton's face dented with a small, worried frown. "What do you need that for?"

"It's for a school assignment," said Olive, semi-truthfully. "We're supposed to bring in old portraits of families."

"Oh," said Morton. The small frown didn't go away.

"I'll take good care of it, I promise," said Olive. "And I'll bring it back as soon as I'm done."

Without another word, Morton turned away. The hem of his long white nightshirt brushed the floorboards as he walked across the porch, between his neighbors, and through the house's front door. He didn't invite Olive inside.

Olive hovered on the porch, clutching the sheaf of papers. The neighbors' painted eyes watched her. "I'll be careful," she promised again, even though no one had spoken. Then she shut up and waited for Morton.

A moment later, he slipped back through the door and thrust the photograph into Olive's hand.

"Thank you," she told him. "I'll keep it safe. I'll keep *all* these things safe." Then, feeling like someone taking a midnight shortcut through a graveyard, Olive leaped down the porch steps and ran across the lawn, into the dark, deserted street. When she glanced over her shoulder one last time, she could see Morton's eyes still following her, even as the mist thickened between them.

Olive toppled back through the frame into the hall, pinning the sheaf of precious papers to her chest with one arm and trying to catch herself with the other. Instead, she landed with a loud "*Ooof!*" on her stomach. She hadn't even had time to roll over before a voice hissed, "Freeze! Present identification!"

Olive tilted her head and looked up into a pair of manic green eyes. The reassembled papers and the photograph were trapped underneath her body. She was quite sure that they were safe from Harvey's sight, but her heart started thumping like a bass drum anyway.

"It's—it's just me," she stammered.

"Ah. Agent Olive." Harvey sat down beside her head and spoke into his imaginary transistor watch. "Suspect intercepted. She's one of ours." His eyes zinged back to Olive's face. "All clear in the yard, under and above ground. However," he went on, lowering his voice, "it is my obligation to inform you that Agent 411 has ascertained that some of the jars are indeed missing."

"Agent 411? Do you mean Leopold?"

Harvey glanced over both of his yellow-painted shoulders before giving a short nod. "Our current objective is to prevent the loss of any more materials."

"Good," said Olive. "But shouldn't you be . . . um . . . monitoring the . . . parameters?" Olive wasn't sure that this was quite the right word, but it appeared to be close enough for Harvey.

"Absolutely correct, Agent Olive. I'll complete another survey of the territory. Over and under. In and out." With another nod, Harvey bolted down the stairs.

Olive rolled over. She pulled the spectacles off her nose and tucked them carefully down the front of her shirt. Then she slid the photograph into her pocket. The house was quiet, but she didn't want to be startled again with the pile of papers in her hands. She needed a place to hide them—someplace *safe,* someplace Annabelle couldn't get at them— where they could wait until she had time to experiment. Just in case Agent 1-800 surprised her again, Olive tucked the papers inside her shirt, where they scratched and tickled softly against her skin. Then she glanced around the hallway.

She wasn't going to hide the pages inside the painting of the moonlit forest. No way. Even the thought of that place made her shudder. She wasn't going to hide them beside the silvery lake either. She couldn't leave them in the painting of the bowl of weird fruit; that would be like playing hide-and-seek in a room with only one piece of furniture. Olive shuffled past the bowl of fruit and neared the craggy hillside with its tiny, distant church.

Before she'd reached the edge of the frame, something in the air seemed to change. Olive sniffed. The air in this part of the hall usually smelled like dust and old wood, with the faint scents of potpourri and mothballs from the guest rooms woven in. But what Olive smelled now was smoke.

Wood smoke. The smell of a cozy log fire in an old fireplace.

She turned toward the painting. A single golden leaf was dancing along the hillside, twirling and leaping, looking absolutely delighted with itself and its world. And Olive wasn't wearing the spectacles.

She stepped closer to the canvas, inhaling the spicy, smoky scent that was drifting from inside. At the edges of the painting, a furze of trees could be seen, their golden leaves as soft as feathers. And today, the bracken that covered the hillside didn't look thorny and brown—it had blossomed into an ocean of tiny pink and white flowers. How had she never noticed how beautiful this place was?

Olive put on the spectacles. This time, instead of a flock of birds, a rich swirl of golden leaves blew across the hillside, whirling and tumbling through the air. A sense of certainty filled her. This wasn't just a perfect place to hide things. This was where she was *meant* to hide things. Olive wrapped her hands around the bottom of the frame and—

"Olive?"

Olive clapped her arms protectively against her body. The papers in her shirt made a muffled crackle.

Horatio stepped through the doorway of the pink bedroom, gazing up at her. His tail flicked back and forth like a fuzzy metronome. "What are you up to?" he asked.

"Just . . . just checking things," Olive stammered. "Making sure everything is safe."

Horatio's sharp eyes moved across her face. "You look . . . How shall I put this?" He gave her a little smile. "The expression 'like the cat who ate the canary' comes to mind, but I've always found it rather prejudiced. No, you look like the girl who ate the forbidden cake, and ended up with a streak of chocolate across her chin."

"I got a bad grade on a math quiz today," Olive improvised quite honestly, standing as still as she could in hopes that the papers wouldn't crinkle again. "I was thinking about hiding it in there."

Horatio's eyes flicked from Olive's face to the painting. "In *there?*" The cat seemed to hesitate. "I wouldn't suggest that. In fact, I would suggest avoiding that painting altogether." With a swish of his tail, Horatio glided abruptly past her.

"What?" said Olive, gazing after him. "But why?"

Horatio ignored her.

"*Why?* You can tell me, Horatio. You can *trust* me."

At this, Horatio paused. He turned to meet her eyes. "Olive, why don't you go wash up," he said dryly. "You've got some guilt on your face."

Then, with another tail-swish, Horatio disappeared through a darkened doorway.

9

As IT TURNED out, Olive didn't find a clever place to hide the paint-making papers that night. Unless you think your own backpack is a clever place to hide things. And Olive didn't.

Having the papers inside her backpack meant that Olive had to carry the backpack with her everywhere: to the dinner table, to the bathroom, to bed—and the next day, through the crowded halls of junior high, where the effort of avoiding Rutherford would have been trouble enough. It meant that she felt paranoid and preoccupied and even-more-than-usually jumpy. It also meant that she had to keep at least a part of her mind on the safety of the backpack, rather than devoting *all* of it to imaginary screaming matches with Rutherford. But there was plenty of room left over.

Why had she let herself start to count on an outsider like Ruth-erford Dewey? Olive fumed as she slammed her locked door. *What was the point of making friends if they were just going to zoom away to schools in Sweden as soon as you were sure they were your friends in the first place?* She was just glad she *hadn't* told him about the paints or the papers. It would be enough bother weeding him out of her life as it was.

Olive dragged these angry thoughts through every hour of the school day, until at last she was hauling both them *and* her backpack up the gritty stone staircase to the art room.

"Attention, everyone!" Ms. Teedlebaum called, attempting to blow on her dangling whistle necklace and blowing on a ballpoint pen necklace instead. "Settle down and take out the photographs I asked you to bring."

While the students obeyed, Ms. Teedlebaum, who was barefoot that day for one reason or another, taped a large photograph to the chalkboard. A hush fell over the room as, one by one, the students noticed the picture. Olive, sensing the sudden silence, stopped scowling down at her tabletop and looked up at the photograph.

It was a family portrait. Judging by the kinky red hair on everyone's head, it was a *Teedlebaum* family portrait. Six family members—a mother and father, two boys and two girls, one of whom must have been the young Ms. Teedlebaum—posed in front of a large fireplace. All six of them were in costume. The mother and four children were dressed as logs, their arms and faces poking out of holes cut in painted cardboard tubes. The father, on the other hand, was dressed as an axe.

No one in the class spoke, but as everyone looked at the photograph, a palpable air of unease filled the room. Behind the smiling Teedlebaum faces lay the implication that Father Axe was going to *chop up* the rest of his family—chop them up, and then perhaps toss them on the fire that flared cheerily behind them.

A boy near the front of the room tentatively raised his hand. "That's your family, right?"

"Yes," said Ms. Teedlebaum. She glanced up from the pencil she was twisting in the sharpener around her neck. "That's us, about twenty years ago."

"Why—why are you . . ." stammered a boy in a much-too-large sweater who sat to Olive's left. "Why—"

"Why are you all dressed like that?" The girl in eyeliner took over.

"My father ran a lumberyard," said Ms. Teedlebaum, setting up a giant sketchpad next to the photo.

"Was it Halloween?" asked the girl.

"No," said Ms. Teedlebaum. "All right, everyone. When you start sketching from a photograph, you want to look at the big picture. Get a sense of scale." Ms. Teedlebaum turned toward the giant sketchbook and began to draw. "See how I'm sketching six ovals for the faces? You can tell that I'm planning to fill the whole page. Now I'll make a very simple outline of the bodies." Ms. Teedlebaum drew the shapes of five logs and one axe, her pencil making soft hissing noises against the paper. "You can always erase any lines you don't need later. Once you've got those outlines, you can start adding the details." Ms. Teedlebaum tossed her pencil into the chalkboard tray. It sent up a little puff of powdery white dust. "We'll be painting these eventually, but we're going to sketch before we paint. Just like you have to learn to roller skate before you can ski. As for materials," Ms. Teedlebaum went on as the students blinked at each other, "if you need another pencil or eraser or a new sheet of paper, just look around the room. They're scattered everywhere. You should be able to find what you need if you look under enough other things." With a smile that seemed to suggest she'd just said something very wise, Ms. Teedlebaum clinked and jangled across the room to her desk.

Olive looked back down at the photograph of Morton's family. Then she picked up her pencil and slowly made two large circles on her sheet of paper. Morton was already in a painting; he didn't need to be in another one. And creating another portrait of Lucinda Nivens could mean a whole houseful of trouble, as Olive was well aware. Her portrait was going to contain just two people.

Frowning at the photo, Olive settled down to work. As she drew, a teeny bit of her fury and fear seemed to trail out through the tip of her pencil, and Olive wondered if she might finally be able to turn all of this trouble into something worthwhile.

Olive tried to keep her mind on her project as she boarded the bus that afternoon. Rutherford was sitting in their usual seat near the front, but Olive marched right past him, plunking down in a seat several rows farther back. From the corner of her eye, she saw his head poke into the aisle, his smudged glasses swiveling in her direction. She turned toward the window.

When the bus ground to a stop at the foot of Linden Street, Olive bolted up the aisle and hit the sidewalk at a run before Rutherford could make it to the steps.

"Olive!" she heard him shouting after her. "Olive, wait! You're making a mistake!"

But Olive didn't even give him a glance.

She wasn't making a mistake about Rutherford. *He* was the one making a mistake if he thought she'd listen to him now.

Blinking away a few irritating tears, Olive slammed through the house's heavy front door and locked it behind her.

The silence within the old stone walls flooded over her like water. Her breath seemed suddenly, shockingly loud. For a moment, she thought she'd caught the sound of muffled footsteps, running across the floorboards above—but then she realized that this was just her own speeding heartbeat. Clutching the spectacles with one hand and her backpack with the other, Olive rushed up the stairs to her bedroom.

With the jars of ingredients in her arms, she craned back out into the hall. Open doorways gaped at her. Picture frames gleamed in the afternoon light. Keeping watch for any glimmering green eyes, Olive darted back down the stairs and along the hallway to the kitchen.

She arranged her materials on the scarred wooden countertop. Five mixing bowls. Five spoons. Five dusty jars. By a beam of sunlight that flickered with the shadows of windblown leaves, she skimmed the writing on the reassembled pages, matching recipes to ingredients.

Black and white were easy to identify. According to what Olive had learned from the labels on crayons (and Olive could have earned a degree in crayons, with a minor in colored pencils), the shade of blue in the jar standing before her was *Indigo*. The yellow was plain old *Yellow*. The red in the jar must be *Crimson*. Olive bent down to study the thorny script.

Crimson, it read. *Two spoonfuls of dried and powdered blood (goat or cattle), mixed with the ground wings of ladybugs and the petals of one red rose, once the blossom has opened but not a single petal has fallen. Sprinkle with the herb Angel's Tongue. Stir in a stream of fresh blood.*

Olive moved the red jar into a beam of sunlight, turning it around and around. As far as she could tell, its contents *could* be powdered blood and ladybug's wings. Maybe the rose petals were already mixed in too. She unscrewed the crusty lid and took a cautious sniff. She smelled rust and dirt . . . and, underneath, something faintly sweet. She would just assume the petals *were* there—it made everything simpler. As for *Angel's Tongue* . . . Olive had no idea what that would look like, so it could easily be in the jar as well. Besides, the instructions said it was an herb, so it couldn't be too important. Mr. Dunwoody always added rosemary to his roast potatoes, but in Olive's opinion, potatoes were just as delicious all by themselves.

Stir in a stream of fresh blood . . .

Where could she get fresh blood? Olive looked down at her own arms. The faint blue lines of her veins seemed to grow even fainter. Was she brave enough to take a knife from the drawer and—

No. She definitely wasn't.

Olive let out a frustrated growl. She couldn't afford to waste any more time. The cats could appear at any second. And if she didn't want to lose her last human—or sort-of human—friend, she had to think of something . . .

And then, in her mind, a wish collided with a memory like a firework touching a match. Olive skidded across the kitchen and yanked open the refrigerator door. A slab of beef, wrapped in grocery store plastic, sat there on its little foam tray. And the tray was pooled with blood. She scooped some red powder from the jar into the first mixing bowl, poured the blood from the meat over the powder, and stirred. Perfect.

She moved on to the next recipe. *Yellow* called for the yolk of a robin's egg. Olive didn't have any robin's eggs, so she used a regular egg from the refrigerator instead. A chicken's egg yolk would be bigger than a robin's egg yolk, anyway, which meant even more yellow paint. It couldn't have worked out better if she'd planned it.

She was still stirring the thick yellow concoction when a chilly feeling, like a fragment of melting ice, trickled slowly down her spine. The hairs on her neck began to prickle. Olive whipped around, looking in all directions.

She was alone in the kitchen.

But in the window above the old stone sink, where tendrils of ivy made a leafy curtain, she thought she caught the flash of movement. Had someone been watching her?

Olive edged closer to the window. If someone had been there—a man or a woman, a painting, a cat, or a traitor in dirty glasses—that someone wasn't there anymore. The ivy leaves twitched softly in the breeze.

Racing now, Olive spun back to the counter. The white paint's instructions called for milk from a black sheep. Well, Olive reasoned, milk from a black sheep couldn't be too different from milk from a black-and-white cow. She grabbed the jug of two percent from the fridge and sloshed it into the bowl. She hustled along the row, making clever substitutions wherever necessary. *Salt dried from a child's tears?* The salt that came in little paper packets at drive-thru restaurants should be fine. *Water that hasn't run through any pipe?* The bottle in the refrigerator said "Spring Water." That should be good enough.

There. She was finished.

Hands shaking, Olive piled the bowls of paint, the jars, and the instructions onto a big metal cookie sheet. With a last wary glance at the window, she hustled out of the kitchen, carrying her materials with her.

Upstairs, Olive closed her bedroom door and double-checked to make sure that the latch had caught. Then she sat down on the bed, laying out her tools: the photograph of Morton's family, a blank canvas from her art supply drawer, a handful of brushes, and the tray covered with fresh-made paints. As she picked up a pointed brush, she was struck by a new thought. If the painting of Morton's parents turned out well, then she could use these paints to create something—or someone—else. And if that someone happened to be *Rutherford* . . .

Then he wouldn't leave her. He would stay here in this house forever, waiting for her, never changing, only able to come out of his painting when Olive felt like releasing him, just like—

Morton's round, pale face flashed across Olive's mind.

Olive's stomach performed a sickening little twirl. *No.* She wasn't going to use these paints as Aldous McMartin had used them. She was going to *help* people. That was all. With a steadying breath, Olive dipped her brush into the bowl of black paint and got to work.

More than an hour had passed before her concentration was broken by a slamming door.

"Hello!" called her father's cheery voice from the bottom of the stairs. "Is there a sixth-grade student in this house who would like to request specific toppings on her third of a delivery pizza?"

"Yes!" Olive shouted back. Covering the bowls of paint with a damp washcloth and setting her gummy brushes on the cookie sheet, Olive galloped down the stairs.

"How was school today?" asked her mother, turning away from the cupboard as Olive skidded along the hall and through the kitchen door.

"Okay," said Olive, surreptitiously brushing a trail

of salt off of the countertop and onto the floor. "But I have a lot of homework."

Mrs. Dunwoody's face lit up. "Homework?" she repeated, setting three plates on the counter.

"Anything we can help with?" asked Mr. Dunwoody eagerly.

"It's for art class," said Olive.

Her parents' faces fell.

"Well, sometimes art requires math too," Mr. Dunwoody soldiered on. "There are issues of perspective and vanishing points and parallel lines . . ."

"It's a portrait, so there aren't really any straight lines," said Olive as her parents' faces fell again. "And I can do it on my own. But thank you." Then, before her mother could ask her to, Olive picked up the plates and a stack of napkins and went into the dining room to set the table.

Mrs. Dunwoody smiled after her. "Who would have hypothesized that *we* would produce an artist?" she asked Mr. Dunwoody, under her breath.

"It must have been a recessive trait." Mr. Dunwoody smiled back. "I would classify it as a pleasant surprise."

But both Mr. and Mrs. Dunwoody would have been far more surprised if they had known just what kind of artwork was waiting on their daughter's bed, its streaks and spots of paint already beginning to dry.

OLIVE WOKE UP the next morning feeling fine. In fact, she felt better than fine. She felt as if her whole body had been filled with helium, and if she had jumped out of her bedroom window just then, she could have soared out over Linden Street, looking down at the tops of the green and golden trees while the soft autumn wind whipped through her hair.

Under her breath, she practiced her best sickly moan. "Oooooh," she groaned. "Oooooow."

Across the room, leaning against her vanity mirror, stood the half-finished portrait of Morton's parents. Last night, Olive had wolfed down her third of the pizza and barreled back up the stairs before her parents had finished their first slice. She had labored over the painting for the rest of the evening, filling in the lines of old-fashioned clothes, shading arms and hands and necks and fingers until her father had tapped at her door and told her that it was fifty-three minutes past her bedtime. She had been so absorbed that she had nearly forgotten about her troubles with Rutherford. Even Annabelle had started to seem unimportant, like a hornet stuck safely on the other side of a closed screen door.

All she needed was a few more hours to finish the portrait.

Olive slid the spectacles out of her pajama collar and placed them on her nose. The figures in the painting shifted slightly, turning their featureless faces one way and then the other. Olive quickly tugged the spectacles off again—first, because the blank, moving faces were a bit creepy, and second, because she wanted to postpone the excitement of seeing Morton's parents come back to life for good, at last. Of course, they wouldn't be his *real* parents, Olive admitted to herself. She still hadn't found the *real* versions, if they were anywhere to be found. But these parents would be something just as good—or maybe even better. If Olive had mixed the paints correctly, they would be just like Annabelle's living portrait, complete with thoughts, personalities, and memories, but undying and unchanging. Just like Morton himself.

Olive leaned back against the pillows, listening to

the voices at the other end of the hall. Her parents were still in their own bedroom, getting ready for another day crammed with equations and solutions.

She moaned again, loudly this time.

"Mmmmoooooaaaah," she groaned, holding her stomach. "Aaaaaaooooow."

The voices at the end of the hall stopped speaking. A moment later, Olive heard her mother's footsteps tapping along the hall.

There was a soft knock. "Olive?" said Mrs. Dunwoody. The door creaked open, and her mother's face appeared in the gap. "Are you all right?"

"I don't feel so good," Olive mumbled.

"What's wrong?"

"My stomach. And my head. I feel all achy," Olive moaned, squinching her eyes shut. "Maybe it was that pizza."

"Well, you did eat it awfully quickly." Mrs. Dunwoody sat down on the edge of the bed. She pressed her cool palm to Olive's forehead, which felt nice even though Olive didn't have a fever.

"I don't think . . ." said Olive, pretending to run out of breath, ". . . I don't think . . . that I can make it . . . to school today." She peeped through her eyelashes at Mrs. Dunwoody.

Her mother nodded. "I'll call the math department and let them know that I won't be coming in. With this late notice, they'll have to cancel my classes, but—"

Olive's eyes popped open. "No!" she said, much too healthily. "I mean . . . *no* . . ." she groaned, making her eyelids droop again. "You don't have to do that. You should go to work. I'll be fine here by myself. I just want to stay in bed and sleep."

Mrs. Dunwoody frowned. "I don't want to leave you at home alone if you're feeling sick."

"I think it's just the pizza. Really. If I start feeling worse, I'll call your office right away, I promise."

Mrs. Dunwoody's frown remained firmly in place. "Wouldn't you like me to call Mrs. Dewey and ask her to come over to stay with you?"

"NO!" Olive nearly shouted. Then she flopped back on the pillows, hoping that she looked exhausted by the effort of nearly shouting. "I'll be fine here," she panted. "I just want to be by myself." Beneath her lowered lashes, she glanced at the painting. Morton's father's head looked a little lopsided. She would have to fix that.

Mrs. Dunwoody rose slowly to her feet. "Well . . ." she said reluctantly, "I'm done with my classes at noon on Fridays. I'll come straight home afterward, which means I should be here by twelve eighteen."

Olive gave her mother a weak little smile. "Okay."

"But if you start feeling worse, you call me *and* Mrs. Dewey immediately. Agreed?"

"Agreed," said Olive, closing her eyes.

"Get some rest," Mrs. Dunwoody whispered. "We'll lock the doors. Don't let anyone in."

A ripple of fear washed through Olive's stomach, and for a split second, she actually *did* feel nauseous. "I won't," she whispered back.

The bedroom door gave a click. Olive held still, clutching the covers, while downstairs, the coffee maker hissed and two briefcases thumped and finally the heavy front door banged shut. She waited until she heard the car rumble softly away down Linden Street.

With a bounce, Olive sat up and kicked off the covers. She raced across the room to the canvas, too intent on the adventure ahead of her to remember to jump off of the mattress or to check under the bed. Her own smiling face glowed back at her from the vanity mirror. She checked the contents of the cookie sheet, still covered by the damp washcloth. The paints in their bowls looked thicker than they had yesterday, but they weren't yet dry. Olive glanced at the clock beside her bed. She had just over five—no, four—hours until her mother would come home. She had to work fast.

Olive darted back and forth between the vanity and the bedside table, arranging brushes, paints, and canvas. Then she hopped back on top of the bedspread and lifted the canvas into her lap. Olive mixed a batch of peachy-brown paint and settled down to work.

She had straightened the man's slightly crooked head and was just beginning to outline his nose when the hairs on her neck gave a little prickle. Olive felt a zing of worry shoot through her body.

She was being watched.

Slowly, she turned her head toward the bedroom door—the door she *knew* had been closed just moments before—and found herself staring into a single bright green eye. Where another bright green eye should have been, there was only a small leather eye patch. Captain Blackpaw had come to visit.

As sneakily as she could manage, Olive tossed the damp cloth back over the contents of the cookie sheet. "Harvey!" she gasped. "You startled me."

"Aye," the cat snarled proudly. "Any landlubber would be startled at the sight of the fearsome Captain Blackpaw."

"Mmm," said Olive.

"And what be ye doing abed so late on this fine Friday morning?" asked the cat, tilting his head.

Olive sidestepped the question. "You know that it's Friday?" she asked. Often, Harvey didn't seem to be aware of what *century* it was, let alone what day of the week.

"'Course I know that," said Harvey. "'Tis Friday, the ninth of September, 1725."

Yes. There it was.

Olive thought about telling Harvey that there was no school today, or that she had been grounded and forbidden to leave her own room, or that a band of marauding polar bears who only ate sixth graders had been spotted in the neighborhood. But in the end, she decided to stick with the lie that had worked once already. "I'm not feeling too good today," she said. "I think I'm sick." Then she added a small cough for good measure.

Harvey's uncovered eye widened. "Scurvy?" he asked hopefully.

Olive shook her head.

"The itch? The pox?"

"I think it's just bad pizza."

Harvey looked confused.

"Well . . . I'd better get back to resting," said Olive, plumping her pillows in a hinting sort of way.

"Indeed," said Harvey. "If ye need me, raise the flag and fire the cannons." He bounded back through the door with a piratical flourish, shouting, "Captain Blackpaw sets sail for the cove!" A moment later, the sound of running paws had receded down the hallway.

Olive got up and closed the bedroom door again. Then she returned to work on the painting.

She worked until the bowls of paint were nearly empty and her fingers were cramped from holding the brush. Her neck had a funny crick in it, and her face hurt, probably because she'd been smiling back at the people in the painting the entire time. But the portrait was finished. Gazing up at her from the canvas were two painted people in old-fashioned clothes, proudly displaying all the limbs, feet, and fingers that any two real people ought to have. Olive looked from the photograph to the painting yet again. Yes, she had done an awfully good job, if she did say so herself.

She spent fifteen minutes pointing a hairdryer at the canvas, until the paint had gone from shiny and wet to less-shiny and dry. Olive reached out with the tip of her littlest finger and touched the canvas. No paint came off on her skin. The portrait was done.

With a flood of excited bubbles fizzing through her fingertips, Olive settled the spectacles on her nose. Then she tilted the canvas up against her pillows, climbed onto her knees, and got ready to meet Morton's parents for the very first time.

THE SURFACE OF the canvas smooshed and dimpled around Olive's face. To someone who had never pushed her face into a painting, this might have felt abnormal. To Olive, it not only felt normal, it felt *delightful*. It meant that her painting was working. She had done it right. As though she were diving through a doorway made of warm Jell-O, Olive squished her body into the canvas.

One moment, she was crawling across her own rumpled bedspread. The next moment, her hands and knees were scraping against the rough surface of a canvas floor. Being short on time, Olive hadn't painted much of a background for Morton's parents. The room they waited in — if you could call it a room — was just an off-white square of slightly crooked lines.

But the background didn't matter. All that mattered was that Morton's parents were there, smiling and posing, just as Olive had painted them. Their eyes followed her as she got up off her knees and stepped closer.

"Hello," she said shyly. "You're—um—you're Mr. and Mrs. Nivens, aren't you? You're Morton and Lucinda's parents?"

The smiles on the painted faces didn't waver.

"I'm Olive. Morton is my friend."

Olive waited for Morton's parents to answer. Morton's father took his hand off of his wife's shoulder, where Olive had painted it. Now that both arms were dangling at his sides, Olive realized that one was stumpier than the other. And it wasn't just a little bit stumpier. It was a lot stumpier. Olive always did have trouble with foreshortening.

Morton's mother merely stared at Olive, her smile affixed to her face like something pinned to a bulletin board.

Neither of them spoke.

"Umm . . ." said Olive. "Morton has always just called you 'Mama' and 'Papa.' Is there something else I should call you? Your first names, maybe? Or is 'Mr. and Mrs. Nivens' all right?"

The painted people didn't answer. But they nodded enthusiastically. Morton's father went on nodding quite a lot longer than was necessary.

Olive took a step closer, studying their smiling faces. She'd made Morton's mother's eyes a touch too big. Olive had a habit of doing that in her artwork. All of her people turned out looking as though there might be at least one lemur hanging on the family tree. And, if she was honest with herself, Morton's father's neck was just a smidgeon too short. If she was really, *really* honest, she might admit that his collar appeared to be trying to swallow his head. But his *face* was fine, Olive assured herself. The features looked just like they had in the photograph. Morton would recognize him. He would recognize them both. He would be so happy to see them.

"If you'll come with me, I'll take you to Morton. He still lives in your old house. Sort of." Olive struggled on while the portraits watched her, smiling and staring. "So, if you could just hold each other's hands and follow me . . ."

Morton's mother tottered unsteadily forward. Olive suspected that she had made Mrs. Nivens's lower half a bit too long, as she often did in drawings where there was a trailing, puffy skirt involved. And perhaps the ruffled silk of the skirt had come out rather stiff . . . but it was hard to paint realistic-looking cloth. Olive eyed her work, trying to convince herself that Mrs. Nivens *didn't* look like a big black funnel with a head and torso dribbling backward out of the top.

She glanced at Morton's father. Fortunately, he was already standing, and his legs didn't seem to be too long for the rest of his body. However, Olive had forgotten to paint the outline of knees inside the solid black tubes of his pants. When he stepped toward Olive, he had to swing from one straight leg to the other, like a pair of walking chopsticks.

"Okay," said Olive, in a voice that had gotten a bit wobbly. "Now hold on to my hand, and hang on to each other, and do what I do. We have to move fast."

Olive reached out toward Morton's father. He took her hand in his big painted one. There wasn't time to study it for long, but Olive noticed that his hand looked a bit stiff and sausagey, with all its fingers poking out in different directions, like the limbs of a starfish.

Holding on to the portrait's hand, Olive crawled back out of the canvas and onto her squishy mattress. Morton's parents followed her without too much trouble, although his mother did have to squirm a bit to get her massive skirts through. Olive tugged them both across her bedroom and into the upstairs hall.

There, standing in the dusty beams of daylight just outside the painting of Linden Street, Olive got her first clear look at her handiwork. And, as she looked, the realization flooded over her that what looks fine in a painting might be *terrifying* in real life.

The portraits' faces were uneven and askew. They

were flat where they should have been rounded. They were bumpy where they should have been smooth. Their limbs were rigid and awkwardly angled. Morton's mother's eyes, which had looked just a little bit too large from farther away, looked gigantic up close. Their color was flat, dark, and empty, without a reflective spark of light to bring them to life. And Morton's father's mustache, which Olive had formed with such careful brushstrokes, didn't look like hair at all. Instead, it looked like some small, furry animal that had collapsed beneath his nose, but which might regain consciousness at any moment. Olive wasn't sure if it was how she had mixed the paints, or if it was simply her lack of artistic skill, but even the hues of their skin and hair seemed impossibly bright, inhuman, and *wrong*.

She swallowed hard.

This was the best that she could do. Perhaps she was just being picky. Olive knew that she was always her own harshest critic. Even the time when she'd won the purple Grand Champion ribbon at a school art fair during third grade, Olive hadn't felt happy at all—she had only seen the gap in the middle of her masterpiece where one macaroni noodle had come unglued. Maybe Morton would think that his parents looked fine. Maybe they had been a bit lopsided and bumpy in real life. And having parents—even lopsided, bumpy ones—was better than having no parents at all.

"Hang on tight," Olive told Morton's father in a shaky voice. She climbed over the edge of the picture frame, pulling her painted companions with her.

With a sinking feeling in her stomach, Olive led Morton's parents up the misty hill toward Linden Street. The sounds of shuffling and clomping that came from behind her only made the sinking feeling worse. Morton's neighbors peered out from their windows and porches, their once friendly faces now watchful and wary. By the time the trio had reached Morton's tall gray house, the sinking feeling in Olive's stomach had turned into the kind of watery tornado that forms around the drain of a very full bathtub.

Morton was seated on his porch railing, trying to keep his balance while kicking his legs and rocking back and forth. When he spotted the three of them, he froze so abruptly that he almost slid off the railing into the tulip patch. As they got closer, Olive could see that Morton had put on the big T-shirt she had used to carry the torn papers over the top of his nightshirt. The T-shirt belonged to Mr. Dunwoody. *I've got logarithm*, said the front. Olive knew that if Morton turned around, she would see the words *Who could ask for anything more?* printed across his shoulder blades. But Morton didn't turn around. He stared directly at his three visitors as he teetered forward from the railing onto the lawn. Then he shuffled very slowly toward the sidewalk.

"Hi, Morton," said Olive. Her heart gave a little leap—whether from nervousness or hope, the rest of Olive wasn't sure. "I brought you something. And I didn't need three whole months to get it either."

Morton stopped a few feet away. He stared up at the two painted people. Their smiles were fixed in place. Their mismatched limbs hung stiffly at their sides.

"Here's Morton," Olive told them.

Mr. Nivens's face seemed to be fighting against itself. "Arrrr," he said. But his mouth didn't move the way an ordinary mouth would. Instead, it twitched sideways, while the teeth remained clenched. "Raaaa. Ara. Reeeee."

"Mmmmmm," said the painting of Morton's mother. It looked as though she was trying to speak with her lips closed. "MmmmmMMMMmmmmm."

Olive glanced back and forth between the three family members. Her painted people looked just as they had a moment ago: like two figures from a wax museum who had been briefly microwaved.

Morton, on the other hand, looked horrified.

"Take them away," he whispered, backing toward the porch.

"But—but I painted them for *you*," Olive said, following him. The painted people stayed put. "It's what you wanted. That's why I borrowed the photograph, and why I had you tape all the paint-making instructions back together—so I could use Aldous's paints to bring back your mama and papa."

"Those ARE NOT Mama and Papa!" shouted Morton. He whirled around and bolted into the house, slamming its heavy wooden door behind him. A moment later, Olive saw his round white face peering out at them from the corner of a downstairs window.

Olive turned back to her creations.

"MMMmmmmm," said Morton's mother.

"Rarrrrrrrr," added his father.

WITH THE PAINTED creatures that were definitely *not* Mr. and Mrs. Nivens stowed back in their own canvas, Olive sat on her rumpled bedspread, rocking nervously back and forth. This had been a huge mistake.

Each time she glanced at her painting, another lump of regret dropped into her stomach. She had probably just torn up and stomped on the last shred of Morton's trust. And if the cats knew she had taken the jars and used the paints . . . Olive shuddered. Losing Rutherford was bad enough. Now, thanks to this one stupid painting, she could lose every single friend she had left.

As fast as she could, Olive jumbled all the jars and bowls and brushes onto the cookie sheet, covering them with the cloth. She would dispose of them later. First, she had to decide what to do with the painting. Mr. and Mrs. Nivens's wonky faces stared back at her from their canvas, two witnesses to her guilt. She had to get rid of them. But how?

Turning the painting around for some privacy, Olive changed out of her pajamas into blue jeans and a T-shirt and tied on her tennis shoes. She glanced at the clock. It was 11:13. Too bad she had missed 11:11; she could really have used the wish. Olive closed her eyes and tried to think. She couldn't destroy the painting—not while Morton's parents stared out at her with their too-large, lifeless eyes. It was too gruesome. No. She had to *hide* it. She had to hide it someplace safe, and pleasant, and unexpected.

And, with or without her 11:11 wish, Olive suddenly thought of the perfect hiding spot.

With the canvas under her arm, Olive bolted down the upstairs hall and skidded to a stop in front of the painting of the craggy hill. This time, instead of a flock of birds or a flurry of leaves, she saw the clouds in the painted sky begin to shift until one long, bright finger of sun broke through and landed directly on the roof of the old stone church.

That's where she was meant to hide this painting. Olive knew it. Elsewhere was telling her so.

Olive put on the spectacles. She struggled over the

bottom of the picture frame, hauling the canvas with her, and landed with an almost musical crackle in the bracken on the other side. The hill where she lay was carpeted with ferns and grasses and a low, woody plant bearing tiny pink flowers, which tinted the whole landscape with a rosy glow. The breeze that touched her face was cool, and the air smelled spicy, smoky, and sweet. Birds flew above her, calling softly.

Holding the canvas to her chest, Olive stood up and looked around. Rocky hillsides rolled up and down around her, ending in threads of oak and birch forest, where the leaves had turned to gold. At the crest of the nearest hill, the little church was waiting. Olive ran toward it, loving the soft snapping sound her shoe soles made in the flowering plants.

A tiny graveyard encircled the church, with its worn headstones half submerged in flowers. Olive had never seen a *less* creepy graveyard. It seemed practically friendly, with all the graves gathered in a sociable cluster around the church's stone walls.

The doors of the church stood open. Olive slipped inside and found herself in a long, quiet room lined with wooden benches. Rows of windows let in the glow of painted sunlight. One large stained-glass window, at the far end of the church, cast a shattered rainbow across the floorboards.

Gently, Olive set her painting in the very last pew,

out of sight of the church doors. No one would find it here. It would be safe and sheltered, and her poor, deformed portraits would have something pretty to look at.

Olive straightened up. Maybe it was the fact that she wasn't carrying the painting anymore, but she suddenly felt fifty pounds lighter. She skipped back through the open doors into the white sunlight, taking deep breaths of the spicy air—and found herself face-to-face with a huge orange cat, who was seated imperiously on the top of a tombstone.

"Olive Dunwoody," said Horatio softly, "you are a fool. What's more, you are a stubborn fool, which makes you a *dangerous* fool."

Olive didn't know where to begin. So she began at the ending. "I—I just wanted to give Morton his parents back," she stammered. "If I didn't find them in three months, Morton said he would run away." Horatio merely glared, so Olive went on. "I'm going to burn the paint-making papers. And I'll dump out the stuff in the jars. And I'm never going to use them again. And—"

"What did I tell you?" snapped Horatio, green eyes glittering. He was still using a quiet voice, but he looked as though he would have liked to use a much louder one. "It's bad enough that you would do something as imbecilic as *attempt* to concoct and use Aldous's paints.

But then you add insult to idiocy by disobeying my warning." The cat rose to his feet. "I told you not to come into this particular painting. And what did you do? You came directly into this particular painting." Horatio leaped down from the headstone. "We need to get out of here. *Now.*"

"Okay," said Olive. "But would you please tell me *why?* Because this seemed like a really good place to leave the painting. I know I shouldn't have done it in the first place, but—"

"Shh!" Horatio cut her off. "We cannot discuss this *here.*"

"Why not?" Olive demanded.

"Not here!" Horatio growled, already darting away.

The sky seemed to darken from white to gray as the clouds thickened. The beams of sunlight that touched the church were cut off, one after another, like a cluster of candles being blown out.

"I'm sorry, Horatio," Olive called, following the cat as he raced down the hill. She ran faster and faster, trying to keep up, but Horatio streaked ahead of her. "I know it was stupid," she panted, "but I just wanted to help Morton. I thought I could—"

Olive tripped over a jutting stone. She landed hard on her palms, scraping her skin against the exposed rock. Thorny stems of the flowering plants snagged at her wounds. Blood, even brighter than the blood-red paint waiting in her bedroom, seeped through her torn skin.

Olive looked up. Where Horatio's soft orange fur had glowed through the bracken a moment before, now there was nothing—only a cluster of gray twigs twitching in the wind. Shaking her stinging hands, Olive staggered to her feet again and surveyed the hill. There—far below her, off to her right—she caught the swish of a luxuriant orange tail.

"Horatio, please!" she shouted, running toward the flash of orange fur. "Don't be mad at me!"

There was no answer.

By the time she reached the spot where she'd seen the flash of orange, Horatio was gone. The brush grew thick and wild all around. Ahead of her lay the forest, canopied in brown and gold. She glanced over her shoulder, but she was no longer sure which way led back to the picture frame. The hillsides folded into each other, one identical ridge following another, and the little stone church had vanished from sight.

"Horatio!" Olive yelled as an icy panic rippled through her. "I lost track of the frame!" Her hands throbbed. The bleeding hadn't stopped. A little river of blood was trickling along her lifeline. *"Horatio!"*

From the woods ahead of her there came a soft crackling sound. Olive froze, listening. Between the trunks of trees, she thought she glimpsed another flash of orange. Before it could vanish again, Olive bolted after it, into the forest.

A carpet of brown and gold leaves crunched under her shoes as Olive hurried along, scanning the gray tree trunks. There it was again—a hint of orange fur shifting through the shadows. Olive chased it into the rustling trees. The sky seemed to be growing darker still, and the scent in the air had changed somehow. The flowery smell of the hillsides had been replaced by something sharper and smokier. Olive paused to take a deep breath, scanning the forest all around her for another fuzzy orange splotch. But this time, what she spotted wasn't fuzzy and orange. It was solid and wooden and dark, and it jutted out from behind a cluster of birch trees in the distance. Keeping her leaf-crunching footsteps as light as she could make them, Olive tiptoed nearer.

A tiny cottage, hardly more than a shack, waited for her in a small clearing. Its wooden roof was crooked. Stones had been stacked together haphazardly to form its walls. One huge oak tree towered over it, as though protecting it from above, and a trail of painted smoke wound out of its chimney, twisting on the breeze. The cottage's door was open, and, in the gap left by that open door, Olive caught sight of something orange.

"Horatio!" she shouted, darting to the doorway before the cat could disappear again.

But it wasn't the cat who greeted her.

"**H**ELLO THERE," SAID a man's deep voice.

He stood in the shack's open doorway, with Horatio seated against his shins. He was tall—so tall that his head almost brushed the ceiling of the little cottage—and young, and very slender, with reddish hair and sharp cheekbones and a strong, square jaw. Something about him made Olive think of Robin Hood. Maybe it was his voice, which had an old-fashioned, British-sounding accent . . . or maybe it was the bow and quiver of arrows she could see hanging on his wall just through the open door. It certainly wasn't his clothing. As Olive ventured closer, she could see that the man's pants were patched and torn, and his shirt was stained with soot.

"H-hello," Olive stammered. "That's my cat," she added, pointing at Horatio. "Sort of."

"So he is yours now, is he?" said the young man, smiling. The smile made his face quite handsome, and now he looked even *more* like Robin Hood on a TV show, in spite of his ragged clothes. "I'm glad to hear it. He's had some other owners in the time I've known him."

"Oh . . ." said Olive slowly. "Then he's been in here—I mean, in this painting—to see you before?"

"Oh, yes," said the young man. He reached down to scratch Horatio between the ears. Horatio tilted his head toward the man's hand, his green eyes sliding shut. Olive had seldom seen Horatio look so pet-able. "We've known each other a good long while."

"It looks like it," said Olive, shuffling awkwardly from foot to foot and trying to remember *not* to wipe her bloody hands on her shirt. "Well—I'm sorry to take him away again, but I need him to lead me back to the picture frame." Olive looked from the man to Horatio. The cat gazed back at her calmly. "Horatio," she said, raising her eyebrows in a hinting way, "didn't you say we had to *get out of here?*"

Horatio met her eyes. "There is no hurry," he said. "We're perfectly safe now."

Olive turned to the young man again and gestured toward the hills beyond the edge of the wood. "I know it's kind of silly, but I got lost out there, and now I don't—"

"Child, you're bleeding," the young man interrupted. Very gently, he grabbed her by the wrists and pulled her nearer, turning her palms to get a better look. His hands were very cold, which Olive knew meant that he'd always been a painting, not a trapped and transformed person—like Olive herself would be if she stayed in here for too long. "You'd best let me clean you up," he said.

Olive looked into the man's painted eyes. Other people would probably have called their color *hazel*, but Olive could see that his eyes were actually a mixture of green and amber and gold. Aldous McMartin might have been a very bad man, but he was a very good painter to have made eyes this sparkling and alive. Olive knew just how tricky painting eyes could be.

"It's all right. We are safe here," Horatio said, noticing her hesitation. She glanced from the young man's painted eyes to Horatio's bright green ones, and the cat gave her a reassuring nod.

"Okay," she said at last. "But I can't stay long."

The man nodded, smiling. He drew her inside the tiny cottage.

A small iron stove was burning with painted light in one corner, and sending wisps of painted smoke up through the chimney. It gave off a gentle warmth, and its flickering light reminded Olive of the candles she had seen burning in the windows of the painted Linden Street. But there were too many other things inside the cottage for Olive to think about the fire for long. The walls of its one tiny room were covered with a wild collection: dried bunches of herbs and flowers, carpentry tools, cooking utensils, a little mirror, pots and pans, bits of fur and feathers and cords and strings. It was nearly as jumbled as the attic of the old stone house. But these things were much shabbier and rougher than the antiques in the attic. These were the belongings of someone who didn't even have what he *needed,* let alone enough stuff to fill a whole third floor with the overflow.

"So—you live here? All the time? In this one little room?" Olive asked, before realizing that these questions might sound rather rude and wishing that she could stuff them back in again.

But the man just smiled. He glanced up from the small square table where he was folding a scrap of fabric. "Yes, I do."

"All by yourself?"

The man went on smiling. "That's right. It's just me and a few animal friends." He gestured to the woods outside, where birds and squirrels chittered among the branches. Then he dipped the folded cloth into a jar filled with what looked like water, and patted it softly against Olive's palm.

Olive flinched and bit her lip. But she let the man go on cleaning her skin, even though it stung, and his painted fingers felt as cold as river stones around her hand. She glanced around the shabby little room again, and then back down at the man's bony fingers. She had the sudden urge to bring him some food—and maybe some nice new clothes too—before she remembered that he was a *painting*, not a person who felt cold or hunger at all.

"There," said the man at last. He held up the damp fabric. Olive watched the splotch of water and the red streaks of her blood fade away as the cloth returned to normal.

"So, Olive," he said, tossing down the cloth, which flew back to its regular hook on the wall and straightened itself neatly, "how do you like your new home?"

Olive paused. "How did you know my name?"

The young man blinked. "Horatio told me," he said, after a moment.

Olive glanced down at Horatio, who was looking very comfortable beside the young man's feet, grooming his whiskers. "It's all right, Olive," said the cat, catching her eyes again. "You can trust him."

Something outside of the cottage made a soft thumping sound. Olive looked around, but neither Horatio nor the young man seemed to notice it. Probably just the wind, Olive told herself. "Um . . ." she began. "I'm growing to like it more and more. It's starting to feel like *home*. For a long time, it didn't. I could tell—at least, it seemed like—the house didn't want us here. But now I think maybe it does. A little bit, anyway."

The red-haired man nodded. "Good," he said. He watched her for a moment, smiling and silent. Then he said, "Well, Olive, we'd best get you back to the picture frame, before any other injuries befall you. Horatio, you know the way."

Looking slightly reluctant, the cat got up. He padded to the door and waited, with his eyes on Olive.

"Thank you," said Olive to the young man.

"No, I thank *you* for visiting *me*," said the man, leaning against the door frame to watch them go. In the daylight that fell through the doorway, his reddish hair shone in waves, and his features looked as clean and strong as if they had been carved out of wood. Olive couldn't decide if she thought he was handsome now, or if he just looked like a hawk crossed with a lion.

She waved. The man waved back. Horatio gave him a little nod. Then Olive and the cat set off through the woods.

Maybe it was her guilt—or maybe it was her sense that the man was still staring after them—but Olive didn't speak until they reached the edge of the trees, and the shack had long since disappeared from sight.

"Horatio," she said as they hurried up the first rocky hillside, "who was that man?"

Horatio didn't turn around. "Just a peasant," he said. "A poor man without a real home."

"That's sad," said Olive, remembering the man's gentle, bony hands and ragged cuffs.

"Yes," said Horatio.

Olive let a few silent moments go by. "You're mad at me, aren't you?" she asked as they climbed through the mounds of bracken.

The cat didn't answer.

"I wasn't trying to do anything stupid. I just thought if I made a painting of Morton's parents, then he would stay Elsewhere and be safe, and not be lonely anymore. But it turned out wrong."

"Of course it did," said the cat.

"I won't do it again," said Olive. "I'm going to get rid of the instructions, and I'll dump everything from the jars down the toilet. I'll even throw away all the stuff from the room below the basement, if you think—"

"No," Horatio cut her off. "*I* will take care of the jars and the paint-making instructions. *You* just need to stay out of trouble."

"I'll try. I promise," said Olive. "Do you believe me?"

Horatio gave her a look out of the corner of his eye, but he didn't say anything more.

They trotted down the next hillside, Horatio staying several steps ahead, Olive trying to keep up without tripping over anything. Ahead of them, in the wispy white air, Olive could make out the square of the picture frame glowing with light from the upstairs hall.

Horatio waited below the frame as she put on the spectacles, watching her fumble them in her still sore hands. "You go through first," he commanded, taking a final sweeping glance at the craggy hillsides. "I want to keep an eye on you."

Olive obeyed. She landed on the carpet in the upstairs hall with one arm trapped beneath her and one large orange cat on top of her. "You managed to catch my claw on your cuff," said Horatio in an irritated tone, extracting his paw from the leg of her jeans. Olive felt his chilly claw scrape her ankle as he hopped off of her legs and sidled away. "You could be quite the formidable enemy, Olive, if you managed to inflict any of this sort of damage on *purpose*."

"Are you all right?"

"Yes. Fine," snapped the cat, shaking his paw. "I assume all the painting materials are in your bedroom?"

Olive nodded.

"Then why don't you go downstairs while I take care of them?"

Olive frowned. "But how are you going to—"

"We have *ways*, Olive. Talking is not my only talent."

"Okay." Olive stood up and edged slowly toward the head of the stairs. Horatio's eyes followed her. "I was really going to get rid of everything, Horatio. Are you sure you don't want me to help?"

"If I did, I would have said so," Horatio pointed out. "And if I may remind you, Olive, it has often been better for everyone concerned when you did *not* know exactly where things were. Now *go downstairs.*"

Prodded by Horatio's words, Olive thumped slowly down the steps. She looked back over her shoulder more than once. Each time, she found Horatio still watching her, his green eyes intent and cold.

AFTER BEING BANISHED downstairs by Horatio, Olive shuffled unhappily through the empty rooms, making a dive for the living room couch when she heard her mother's cheery voice call out, "I'm home!" from the front door.

For the next few hours, Olive was stuck under several blankets and Mrs. Dunwoody's close supervision, pretending that her stomach hurt and that her scraped palms didn't. She was too worried about Horatio's anger and Morton's terror to concentrate on a book. Instead, she watched TV until she could feel her brain beginning to melt, and all the storylines ran together, and soon she couldn't remember who had won what talent contest or stolen whose boyfriend or insulted whose family and had to fight in a magical duel.

But sometime in the midafternoon, when the soap operas and talk shows had finally given way to cartoons, there was a sharp tap at the front door.

"I'll get it," said Mrs. Dunwoody, setting down the stack of math tests she was grading. "Don't get up, Olive." She patted Olive on the head on her way out.

Olive craned over the arm of the sofa, leaning as far as she could toward the hallway without toppling straight onto the floor. Her first thought was that it must be Rutherford, and a part of her—a small, mostly hidden part—hoped that it was. Her second thought was that it might be Annabelle herself, perhaps in disguise as a delivery person, hiding her face behind a huge bouquet of flowers. "These are for you," Annabelle would say, and Mrs. Dunwoody would invite her inside, and then the floodgates of *real* trouble would break open . . .

But the voice that came from the front door wasn't Rutherford's *or* Annabelle's.

"Hello," said a voice that was accompanied by the jingling sound of many keys and pens and whistles. "I'm Florence Teedlebaum, the art teacher at the junior high. I noticed that Olive left her project at school, and after I learned your address from the school office, I thought I would drop it off so that she could finish it in time for its due date on Monday."

Olive, still wrapped in blankets, wriggled off the

couch and sidled along the walls toward the entryway, keeping out of sight.

"How nice of you," Mrs. Dunwoody was saying. "I'm Alice Dunwoody, Olive's mother. I know Olive has always enjoyed art class."

"As have I," said Ms. Teedlebaum as Olive slipped across the hall and flattened herself against the staircase so she could peek through the banister. "And what do you do, Olive?"

"Alice," said Mrs. Dunwoody.

"Florence," said Ms. Teedlebaum correctively.

"Florence," Mrs. Dunwoody repeated, after a brief pause. "I'm a mathematician."

"Really!" exclaimed Ms. Teedlebaum. "I've never understood much about math. I just couldn't see the point of adding up the same numbers over and over again when the answers almost always come out just the same, anyway."

"Yes . . ." said Mrs. Dunwoody slowly. "Well, it was so nice of you to come all this way to bring Olive her homework."

Ms. Teedlebaum flapped her hands. Even muffled by the sleeves of her jacket, her bracelets jangled loudly enough for Olive to hear. "Not at all. It was no trouble. I've been to this house before. As a matter of fact, I had a bit of an ulterior motive in driving over here."

"Oh?" said Mrs. Dunwoody.

OH?! echoed a voice in Olive's head.

"Your collection of Aldous McMartin's art," said Ms. Teedlebaum. "It's practically legendary in this town."

Olive's heart rocketed up into her trachea.

"Oh," said Mrs. Dunwoody, "I hardly think of that as *ours*. I'm not sure a person can truly *own* a work of art, anyway. I really think of it as belonging to the house."

Olive swallowed. Her heart slipped a tiny bit lower in her throat.

"Where are my manners?" Mrs. Dunwoody asked. "Come in, please. I'm a rusty hostess. I could count the number of visitors we've had in this house on one hand."

Olive listened with mounting dread as Ms. Teedlebaum's shoes tapped into the foyer. "But I bet you wouldn't need to use your hand, being a mathematician."

Mrs. Dunwoody laughed. "That's very true."

"I've always thought it would be handy to have more fingers, just so you could keep count of more things," said Ms. Teedlebaum.

"I suppose that would be *hand-y*, yes," said Mrs. Dunwoody.

Both women giggled. Olive thought she might be sick.

"Would you like a short tour?" Mrs. Dunwoody asked.

No! No! NO!! chanted the voice in Olive's head.

"Yes!" said Ms. Teedlebaum.

"Let's start in the library." Mrs. Dunwoody ushered her guest toward the heavy double doors. "This is one of my favorite paintings in the house . . ."

The sound of voices and footsteps and jangling keys faded as the two women walked into the room. Olive remained crouched against the staircase, knowing that they were gazing up at the painting of the dancing girls in the flowery meadow. When they moved into the parlor to look at the French street scene, Olive wriggled across the hall, pressing close to the doorway.

"Lovely," she could hear Ms. Teedlebaum saying. "Don't those pigeons look as though they might take flight at any moment?"

They drifted through the dining room and the kitchen, Ms. Teedlebaum gasping and oohing and exclaiming, Olive shuffling surreptitiously behind in her wrapping of blankets. When the women moved toward the stairs, Olive had to hop backward through the parlor doors, hiding in the corner until she heard Ms. Teedlebaum comment on the beautiful light reflected in the silver lake and the details of the bare branches in the moonlit forest.

"There are more down this part of the hall, in the

guest bedrooms," she heard Mrs. Dunwoody saying. The women stepped into the blue bedroom, and Olive waddled as quickly as she could up the staircase, still wrapped like a pupa in her quilted cocoon.

A moment later, Mrs. Dunwoody and Ms. Teedlebaum reemerged, and Olive leaped through her own bedroom door in time to avoid being seen. Even while she eavesdropped on the conversation in the hallway, Olive couldn't help but notice that her room had already been stripped of every trace of her ill-fated artwork. The paints, the jars, the handwritten instructions, and even her paintbrushes had vanished. For someone without opposable thumbs, Horatio had certainly been thorough.

"Look at the colors in this still life," Ms. Teedlebaum was observing. "And what strange fruits. I'm not sure I've seen any of these before."

"I've noticed that too," said Mrs. Dunwoody. "Perhaps they are Victorian varieties that just aren't cultivated anymore."

"Or perhaps they're all mutants," said Ms. Teedlebaum, as if this was a more reasonable explanation.

"Hmm," said Mrs. Dunwoody.

The art teacher jingled into the lavender bedroom, where Annabelle's empty portrait waited. Olive zigged out of her room and into the blue bedroom, crouching behind the door.

"This is interesting," she could hear Ms. Teedlebaum say. "There's a painting in this frame, but there's nothing *in* the painting. It looks like the background was painted, but the foreground was never completed."

"That's strange," Mrs. Dunwoody agreed. "I never noticed that."

"Perhaps the artist was trying to make some sort of statement . . . Something about how what *isn't* there when we expect it to be can be even more powerful than what *is* there."

Olive clutched the doorknob with both hands. Even wrapped in the blankets, her body shuddered with a wave of sudden cold.

The floor creaked as the women stepped back into the hall.

"Is there a third floor?" Ms. Teedlebaum asked. "The house looks so tall, from the outside . . ."

If she hadn't been holding on to the doorknob, Olive might have collapsed completely.

"It's funny you should mention that," said Mrs. Dunwoody. "From the height of the house, it's clear that there *was* a third floor, but its entrance has been walled up or sealed over entirely. We haven't even found the spot where the entrance used to be."

Olive let out the breath she'd been holding. It came through her nose in short, shaky puffs.

"Well, thank you so much for letting me look around.

This has been a real pleasure," said Ms. Teedlebaum, clanking and jingling past the door where Olive hid. Olive watched the puff of kinky red hair descend the staircase, followed by her mother's much-less-puffy head. She waited until she heard two sets of footsteps on the hallway floor below. Then she waddled out into the hall and down the staircase, clutching her blankets, trying to look as though she'd been up in her room being innocently sick the whole time.

Mrs. Dunwoody glanced up as Olive came down the steps.

"Olive, your teacher brought over an art project for you to finish. Wasn't that nice of her?"

"Yes," said Olive, in a sickly croak. "Thank you, Ms. Teedlebaum."

Ms. Teedlebaum smiled and flapped her hands again. "It was nothing. I hope you feel better soon."

"I hope you—" said Olive, in knee-jerk fashion, before catching herself. "Um—feel good too."

Ms. Teedlebaum didn't seem to find this odd. She just went on smiling. Then she wrapped one of her three scarves back around her neck, setting the cords of keys and trinkets clinking, said "Good-bye!" and jangled out the door.

"What a nice woman," said Mrs. Dunwoody, closing it behind her.

Leaning her forehead against the front windows,

Olive watched the art teacher's rusted station wagon bump out of the drive and pull away. Her heartbeat was finally slowing back to its normal rate, but her mind was still whirring along at high speed.

How had Ms. Teedlebaum known about Aldous McMartin's paintings? Was she only interested in them as *art* . . . or was she looking for something more? Olive felt the hairs on the back of her neck rise as a new thought shot across her mind: Did Ms. Teedlebaum have something to do with the note from Annabelle that had been planted in the art classroom?

Olive pressed her face to the cool glass, feeling genuinely sick once again. It was just as Annabelle had written—it was hard to know whom to trust. These days, Olive wondered if it was safe to trust anyone at all.

O N SATURDAY MORNING, a strange thing happened.

It wasn't that Olive managed to find a matching pair
of slippers under her bed, although this *was* unusual.
And it wasn't that she both brushed *and* flossed her
teeth before she tromped downstairs, although this
was also very unusual. It wasn't even that she remembered all the digits of someone else's phone number
when she picked up the receiver and started dialing,
although this was *extremely* unusual. The strange thing
was that the phone number she was dialing was Rutherford's.

Olive dropped the receiver back into its cradle
before it could begin to ring.

What was she thinking? Had she forgotten overnight

that Rutherford was deserting her? Olive stared at the silent telephone, chewing on a strand of her hair. She couldn't depend on him anymore. She couldn't tell him about her horrible mistakes with the paints, or about Ms. Teedlebaum's visit. She would have to face her troubles alone.

Well . . . maybe not *completely* alone.

Inside the painting of Linden Street, Olive scurried up the hill, displacing puffs of mist that settled swiftly back into place. An old woman in a rocking chair stopped rocking as Olive hurried past. Olive gave a little wave. The woman didn't wave back. Through dark windows, Olive could feel other eyes watching her—the same eyes that had watched her yesterday, as she led her deformed portraits to Morton's lawn.

Cheeks burning, Olive tucked her chin to her chest and hurried on.

Morton wasn't in his yard. He wasn't on his front porch either. Olive scanned the street all around the tall gray house, but there was no sign of a small boy in a long white nightshirt. She checked the branches of the oak tree. No Morton. She looked behind the shrubs. No Morton.

The door of the tall gray house was shut. Olive knocked, but there was no answer, and when she tried to turn the doorknob, she found that it was stuck firmly in place. It couldn't be locked, Olive knew, because nothing inside Elsewhere could be changed without changing quickly back. There was only one way the knob could be held in place: If someone inside was doing the holding.

"Morton?" she called softly, putting her lips to the door. "Morton, I know you can hear me. I have something for you."

As soon as the words came out of her mouth, Olive realized that they were probably the *last* words she should have said. Morton wouldn't want any sort of surprises from Olive for a very long time.

The door stayed shut. Morton's whole house was giving her the silent treatment.

Bending down, Olive took the old black-and-white photograph of Morton's family out of her pocket and slipped it carefully through the narrow gap beneath the door.

There was a long, quiet moment while Olive stood on the porch, staring at the door. And then, slowly, it creaked open, and Morton's small white form edged out.

"I thought you might be surprising me with more *parents,*" he said.

Olive gestured to the empty porch. "Nope. No parents. I'm done trying to make anything with Aldous's paints."

Morton hung on the doorknob, swinging slowly

back and forth. His tufty white hair drifted back and forth too, like dandelion seeds that wouldn't blow away. "Do those *cats* know what you did?" he asked.

"What do you mean, *those cats?*" Olive repeated. "You know their names."

Morton only shrugged and went on swinging.

"No," said Olive. "Well—Horatio knows. He was really mad. He took the paints and the papers away."

Morton narrowed his eyes. "Mr. Fitzroy says," he began, swinging back and forth even faster, "he says . . . they might not have our best interests at heart." Morton's words marched out in the stiff pace of something memorized.

"*Mr. Fitzroy* doesn't really know them," Olive said, putting her fists on her hips. "I *told* your neighbors that they could trust the cats."

Morton stopped swinging. His eyes drifted toward Olive's toes. "Well—they don't really trust *you,* either."

Olive's mouth opened, but nothing came out. The neighbors knew she had lied about keeping the papers safe. They knew she had used the paints. She had used the neighbors too, taking advantage of their help—and Morton's—to do something that didn't help anyone at all. They didn't trust her. And she wasn't sure she could blame them.

Morton gazed past Olive's shoulder. "I bet I can balance on this railing better than you," he said abruptly, hopping across the porch and climbing onto its banister.

"I bet you can too," said Olive.

But Morton decided to prove it anyway. He walked back and forth several times, with both skinny arms sticking straight out, and only fell off into the bushes once. Olive clapped politely when he was done.

"I'm glad you're still here, Morton," she said as Morton slid down from the railing.

Morton gave her a frown.

"I mean, I'm not glad that you're *stuck* here, I just . . ." Olive trailed off with a sigh. "You remember Rutherford, from two houses away? You met him when Lucinda was hiding Annabelle in her house." Olive plopped down on the porch steps. "He's leaving. He's going to go to a fancy school in Sweden, where his parents are doing research, and I'm going to be stuck in sixth grade all alone." Olive flicked a fallen oak leaf off of the step and watched it flutter back into its place. "I bet he was just curious about this house. I bet he never actually wanted to be my friend in the first place."

Morton sat down beside her. He tugged at the hem of his nightshirt until it covered his toes. Then he said, "Maybe he just misses his parents."

Olive kicked an acorn cap. A moment later it was back in its spot, as though it had never moved at all.

"You have to stay here for three more months, remember," she said softly. "We made a deal."

"Three months minus three days," said Morton.

They were quiet for a minute. Olive leaned forward, holding her chin in both hands. Morton did the same. They both stared across the street at the silent houses on the other side.

"Do you want to go dance in the ballroom?" Olive asked at last.

"Not really," said Morton.

"Want to play with Baltus?"

Morton shrugged.

"We could explore a new painting. There are some at the other end of the hall that—"

"That's all right," Morton interrupted. "I think I'm just going to stay here."

Slowly, Olive stood up. "Okay," she said, looking down at the top of Morton's tufty white head. "I'll come visit again soon."

The tufts gave a tiny nod.

Olive waited for another minute before turning away and walking across the lawn into the deserted street.

She passed the empty lot where the old stone house would have stood, if Aldous had painted it there, and was shuffling along yet another quiet lawn when a voice said, "Evening, Miss Olive."

Olive jumped. The old man with the beard— Mr. Fitzroy, she remembered—strolled toward her through the mist. He gave her a smile, which was half hidden in the bristly kinks of his beard.

Olive tried to smile back. "Hello," she mumbled.

"Saw you in here not too long ago," said the man. "You were leading those two"—he paused, as though searching for a word—"*people* up the street."

"Oh," said Olive nervously. "Yes." Suddenly she felt dangerously close to crying. She swallowed. "I was just . . ." she began. "I was just trying to make Morton's parents." Olive shrugged, looking down at her feet. "But it went wrong. And I got rid of everything. The paints and the papers and everything."

The old man studied her. Then he nodded. "I think I'll go check on the boy. Maybe stay with him for a while."

"Thank you," said Olive. She looked into the man's painted blue eyes. "You don't have any guesses about what might have happened to Morton's real parents, do you?"

The man let out a slow, sad sigh that twitched the whiskers of his beard. "It's been a long, long time," he said at last. "A very long time. And when there's nothing new to remember . . ." He trailed off, gesturing at the sleepy street beneath its changeless canopy of twilight. "The memory shuts down." He shook his head.

"I don't remember if they disappeared before or after those cats trapped me here. I don't remember the last time I saw them. But I remember that they were good people. Truly *good*." His painted blue eyes got a bit dreamy. "Mary had a way of looking at you that made you tell her the truth. Even if you hadn't planned on telling it." He chuckled. "It could be pretty risky talking to her if you had anything to hide. Maybe that was why the Old Man hated her so much. He couldn't lie to her."

"*Mary?*" Olive repeated, in a breathless whisper. "That was her name?"

The old man's bushy eyebrows rose. "Well, how about that! I remembered something. Mary Nivens. That was it. Mary and . . . *Harold.*" The eyebrows went up even higher. The old man beamed.

Olive beamed back at him. "Mary and Harold."

Still smiling, the old man turned toward Morton's house. Olive turned the other way, wiping her eyes on her sleeve and grinning at the same time.

The next day, after leaving a deck of cards and the puzzle of a picture of puzzle pieces on Morton's empty porch, Olive set off to find the other friends who hadn't betrayed her.

But the cats apparently did not want to be found. Olive tiptoed around the first floor, peering into the shadows beneath the furniture, while inside the library, Mr. and Mrs. Dunwoody performed a cheerful duet on their computer keyboards. There was no trace of Horatio anywhere. She went down to the basement and stared at Leopold's deserted station for several long, chilly minutes, willing him to appear from the tunnel below. He didn't.

When her feet were too cold to wait any longer, Olive wound her way up to the second floor. With every empty room and gaping doorway, Olive's sense of loneliness grew. By the time she'd searched the last guest-less guest room, she felt as hollow as the house itself. She shuffled back down the hall to her own bedroom and pressed her forehead to the cool windowpane, staring down into the backyard. Far below, she could see the jumbled garden, the filled and hidden hole, the crumbling shed . . . and, just inside the line of lilac bushes, a boy with messy brown hair and a yellow dragon on his shirt.

Her heart gave an involuntary little leap.

Almost as though he had sensed her eyes on him, Rutherford leaped up too, and the thick book he'd been reading flopped out of his lap and onto the ground. He waved both arms in a beckoning way. His lips were moving—moving more slowly than usual, fortunately, or Olive wouldn't have been able to read them at all. *Come outside!* he was calling. *Come out!*

Olive froze for a moment, fingers gripping the windowsill. Then she pulled her curtains shut.

She marched along the upstairs hall, away from her own room, away from the backyard and Rutherford standing in it. She turned into to the pink bedroom, putting on the spectacles and pushing through the painting that led to the attic.

Olive climbed the bug-strewn steps and glanced around the room, with its crooked stacks of boxes and dusty, half-covered furniture. The ruddy light of afternoon threaded through the attic's window, glinting on the ring of mirrors and buffing the metal of the small, battered cannon. Olive peeped out the window. Rutherford still stood in the backyard, frowning up at the house, waiting. He was far enough away that she couldn't be sure, but she thought she saw his eyes travel upward to the attic window. His body seemed to deflate slightly, like a week-old party balloon. Then he stooped down, picked up his book, and disappeared into the withering lilac hedge.

Olive felt an unexpected twinge of disappointment. But before the twinge could become an ache, she was startled by the soft clink of glass against wood, somewhere in the shadows to her right.

"Hello?" she called. "Harvey?"

Winding between an old hat rack and an armchair that looked like it was spitting out its stuffing, Olive tiptoed across the room, trying to trace the source of the sound.

There was another, closer, rattle. "Yes. I'm watching you. I know what you've been up to," muttered a voice with a faint British accent.

Olive craned around the side of a musty sewing dummy. There, just a few feet away, was Harvey. He was perched on the edge of Aldous's cloth-covered easel, looking down at something Olive couldn't see.

"Agent 1-800?" she called.

Harvey whirled around. He leaped off of the easel, positioning himself between it and Olive. "Agent Olive," he replied, with a brusque little nod.

"I haven't seen you in days," said Olive. "Where have you been?"

"I'm on the job," said Harvey. "Surveillance. Surreptitious security. Surgical . . . surceasance."

"Oh," said Olive. "Have you seen anything new?"

Harvey squinted one eye. "Perhaps," he said. "But what I *haven't* seen may pose an even greater threat. If you catch my drift."

"I don't," said Olive. She plopped down on the floor, facing the cat.

Harvey maintained his distance. "The work of a secret agent isn't easy," he said softly. "Keeping your ears peeled, your lips open, your eyes sealed."

"I'm sure," said Olive.

"And then there's the issue of trust," Harvey went on. He gazed up into the rafters, eyes sparkling glassily. "Who can trust a cat who doesn't exist? Who can believe the word of a cat whose entire life is a secret?"

"Hmm," said Olive, who could tell that Harvey didn't really want an answer.

"And who can *we* trust, if no one knows *us*?" Harvey's eyes flicked back to Olive. "Imagine a game of chess in which all the pieces are the same color." The eyes began to sparkle wildly. "You cannot be sure which side anyone is on. Double agents. Triple agents. *Quadruple* agents." The eyes widened slightly with each word. "*Dodecahedral agents.*"

"I can see that you're really enjoying this," said Olive.

For a split second, Harvey looked startled. "I—" he began. His whole body seemed to stiffen. "That is— you will have to excuse me, Agent Olive. I must return to my duties."

Olive got reluctantly to her feet. "I suppose I should get out of your way. If you're busy."

"In fact," said Harvey, backing toward the easel once again, "if you visit this area in the future, you may not see me."

Olive frowned. "Why not? Where will you be?"

"Ah," said Harvey. One whiskered eyebrow rose. "Where *will* I be? That is the question. I shall be everywhere and nowhere. Invisible and indivisible. No *double agent* will be a match for me."

"Oh," said Olive. "Then . . . I guess . . . good-bye."

"Good-bye," said Harvey softly.

Olive slumped back down the stairs and out of the attic, feeling more alone than ever.

That was the last she saw of any of the cats until very late that night. And what she saw then didn't make her feel any less alone.

SOMETIME AFTER MIDNIGHT, when the rest of the house was asleep, Olive woke from a bad dream about a huge chessboard where all the pieces were carved out of purple crayons. The shadows of the ash tree's branches rippled and unfurled across her ceiling. One twig tapped softly at her window. At first, Olive wondered if this sound had woken her. But as she lay there, listening, she heard another sound.

It sounded like a voice. But it wasn't her mother's voice, or her father's voice. It was a voice that she couldn't quite place.

Olive slipped both legs out of bed and pushed back the covers with as little crinkling as she could manage. Holding her breath, she leaped off of the mattress and tiptoed toward her bedroom door. The hinges gave a creak as she pulled it open. Olive moved the door as slowly as she could, forming a gap just big enough for her to peep through.

The hallway angled away from her in two directions. One branch led to the staircase, and beyond that, to her parents' closed bedroom door. The other dwindled off toward the lavender, blue, and pink bedrooms, where Olive couldn't see. Faint silver moonlight glanced off of the banisters, turning the staircase railing into a cage of shadows. The picture frames glimmered like treasure sunk to the ocean floor.

The sound had seemed to come from her left, inside one of the empty guest rooms. There was a dull creak from the floorboards as someone moved out into the hallway. Olive couldn't have seen whoever that someone was without sticking her whole head through the door, so instead, she stayed frozen in place, watching and listening with every nerve in her body. Again, she thought she heard the murmur of a low voice, but she couldn't make out the words.

There was a soft whimper. "Shh," someone hissed.

Olive wished that she could press a pause button on her heart. Its pounding in her ears had grown so loud that very little could squeeze past it. Nevertheless, she managed to catch a muffled thump and a creak, as though someone had jumped on the old floorboards. And then everything was still.

Olive stood as if she were frozen, with both hands clutching the doorknob and one wide eye staring through the gap. She stood there for so long, hearing nothing, that she almost managed to convince herself that she had imagined it all. Perhaps what she'd heard had been the house settling, or the TV from her parents' room. This house had ways of tricking you, as Olive knew—of sending sounds echoing through empty rooms until you couldn't tell what had come from where, what was nearby and what was far away, what was real and what was only the trick of your own fear.

But then, as Olive watched, a shadow slipped silently into view. It was stretched and blurred, as moon-shadows are, but it was clearly the shadow of a cat. It darkened as the cat came closer. Its black outline could have belonged to anyone—to any *cat,* that is—but, as Olive waited, one very specific cat's head appeared.

Its orange fur was washed by the moonlight. Its luxuriant whiskers glinted. It trotted nearer, and soon Olive could make out its tufted paws, its sleek coat, and its long, twitching tail, as big around as a baseball bat.

Horatio.

The cat padded soundlessly past her open door. He turned at the staircase, vanishing down the steps into the darkness.

It took a few minutes before Olive's heart and lungs remembered how to work normally again. *We didn't see anything strange,* Olive reminded them. *It isn't unusual for Horatio to be patrolling the house at night. Maybe he was talking to Harvey, or to someone in a painting, or to himself. Maybe no one was talking at all.*

Gently, Olive closed her bedroom door, checked under her bed, and climbed back between the covers. Then she pulled the blankets up to her chin and tried to figure out why she'd felt compelled to hide from Horatio, her *friend* . . . and why the sight of him slipping along the dark hall had filled her with a strange, low thrum of terror.

Monday morning arrived like a skillet falling on a toe.

Olive wasn't ready for it. Half of her brain still refused to return from that strange, dreamy scene in the darkened hallway, when for a time she'd felt sure that she was witnessing something important—something that needed to be figured out. The other half bumbled through the school day, too dazed to notice the hours sliding by.

She didn't hear anything but the bell in math or English class. At lunch time, she hurried past the cafeteria, where she knew Rutherford would be waiting, and ducked into the nurse's office instead, saying that she had a terrible headache and needed to lie down (which wasn't too far from the truth). Science class passed in a gummy blur. Finally, after a lecture in history that made both her brain and her backside fall asleep, Olive let the flood of students carry her along the halls to the art room.

Ms. Teedlebaum stood at the front of the classroom, covered from neck to ankles in something that looked like a paint-spattered doctor's coat. If the doctor who wore it had been a giant. A giant who got dressed backward. The teacher went on arranging several jugs of paint, pouring colorful streams from one jug into another, as the students trickled in. After the bell rang and a few more anticipatory seconds had passed, she finally looked up.

"Okay. You've transferred your sketches to canvas board at this point," said Ms. Teedlebaum, brushing a hank of kinky red hair away from her cheek and leaving a wide blue paint streak in its place. "Today, we'll start painting. First, you'll get your sketches and your canvas board. No scratch that. Get your paints from the front table first. But before you get your paints, you'll need a palette." Here Ms. Teedlebaum held up something that looked like an egg carton for some very flat eggs. "So, get the palette first. But remember, before you get the palette, you need to cover your work surface. So, first, cover, then palette, then . . . Wait," Ms. Teedlebaum interrupted herself. "Did I say to put on a smock first? No? So, *first,* put on a

smock. Second, cover your table. Third, get your palette. Fourth . . ." Ms. Teedlebaum's eyes seemed to
glaze over. She gazed down at the huge jugs of tem-
pera paint directly in front of her. "*Paint*. That's it. Get
your paint. Then your canvas boards. Did I mention
brushes?" she asked the class, blinking around at the sea
of baffled faces. "Never mind. I'll pass out the brushes
while you . . ." Ms. Teedlebaum paused, then appeared
to give up. "While you do all those other things I said.
Get started."

Olive, whose brain had wandered out of the building and across town while Ms. Teedlebaum was speaking, glanced around to see what everyone else was
doing. Once she'd gathered all the materials, she sat
back down at her table and stared at her canvas board
with its sketch of Morton's parents.

"Mary and Harold," she whispered.

"Here you go," Ms. Teedlebaum announced over
Olive's shoulder, dropping a handful of brushes onto
the table. She paused as her eyes traveled over Olive's
work. "That's really quite good," she said, nodding.
The keys around her neck jangled. "You have an excellent eye. Watch out with the foreshortening of this
arm, though." Ms. Teedlebaum nodded and jangled
again. "You've done this before, haven't you?"

Olive's head jerked up. Her startled hand slashed
a streak of lead across Mary Nivens's skirt. "What do
you mean?"

Ms. Teedlebaum's excited eyes stared at her from just a few inches away. Up close, they looked like a mosaic of green and brown glass. "You've done portraits before," she said, smiling at Olive.

"Oh. Yes," said Olive carefully. "But . . . they didn't really turn out right."

Ms. Teedlebaum tipped her head to one side. A moment later, the springy bush of her red hair tipped over too. "Well," she said, "you know what they say about practice and perfection, and one being next to the other." She gazed at Olive's sketch again. "I wouldn't give up if I were you."

A wisp of Ms. Teedlebaum's springy hair brushed against the skin of Olive's neck, as distracting and ticklish as the questions in Olive's mind. What if Ms. Teedlebaum, like Lucinda Nivens, was secretly working for Annabelle? What if Ms. Teedlebaum had let Annabelle into the art room, or even placed Annabelle's note on Olive's shelf? What if she hadn't come to the old stone house for an art tour at all, but to bring information back to Annabelle?

"Um . . . Ms. Teedlebaum . . ." Olive began, forcing the words out before they could beat a retreat to the back of her mind, ". . . what do you know about my house?"

"Your house?" Ms. Teedlebaum repeated.

"Yes. You came over to my house on Friday, to—"

"Oh, the McMartin house!" Ms. Teedlebaum crowed.

"Of course. Well, everyone in town—at least, anyone in town who's interested in art—has heard all about Aldous McMartin, the painter who built it. He was a bit of an eccentric, I guess," she said, pausing to untangle a piece of toilet paper that had gotten caught in the giant clump of keys on her beaded necklace. "He never sold his paintings, never let them be displayed in public . . . and then he died, and left the place to his granddaughter, and then *she* died, and now it all belongs to you. And that's about it, as far as I know."

Olive took a breath. "So did you ever meet—Annabelle?"

"Who?" Ms. Teedlebaum asked, looking confused. Olive had seen this expression on the art teacher's face several times before. As far as she could tell, it wasn't faked.

"His granddaughter."

"Oh, *Ms. McMartin?* I met her once, yes, but she was a very old lady by then. She didn't look much like an Annabelle—more like a Millicent or a Prunella. Or maybe a Gertrude. No one names babies Gertrude anymore, do they?" Ms. Teedlebaum turned away, looking thoughtful. Then she whirled back around so suddenly that Olive dropped her pencil. "Oh—and Alice—"

"It's Olive."

"Right. Olive." Ms. Teedlebaum leaned on the edge

of Olive's table. "Would you mind if I visited your house again sometime? I'd love to do some sketches, study Aldous McMartin's work in a bit more depth."

"I don't know," said Olive quickly. "I'm not sure my parents would—I mean, we're all really busy, and—"

"Of course." Ms. Teedlebaum waved her hands. Rows of silver bracelets chimed sweetly. "I'm sure you have plenty to worry about, after moving into a big old place like that." She smiled. "Maybe another time, Alice."

Olive watched Ms. Teedlebaum wander away. *Plenty to worry about?* Ms. Teedlebaum had no idea.

For one thing, Olive had to be constantly on guard to avoid both Rutherford and Annabelle, either of whom might appear around a bend in the school corridors at any moment. Luckily for Olive, the big brick building provided a number of handy places to hide.

There were the stairwells that led down to the basement, where huge pipes and vents huffed and whined, and which made a useful (if somewhat nerve-racking) spot to eat lunch all by yourself. There was the third-floor hallway that hardly anyone used, where one small sixth grader could scuttle quickly past the supply rooms and offices, breathing the air that smelled permanently of chalk dust and clay. And there was the all-but-forgotten bathroom at the very end of the music hall, with stalls that had been painted so many times, chips in the metal doors looked like bites out of a many-flavored gobstopper.

But as she darted from classroom to classroom, making herself as inconspicuous as she could, part of Olive wished that she could *stop* hiding—that Rutherford would just go away and give her one less thing to hide *from*. She even found herself hoping that Annabelle would simply get it over with, looming out of the shadows to put an end to all of this awful anticipation. This was like a game of hide-and-seek that had gone on much too long. *What was Annabelle waiting for, anyway?*

And then—on Friday—the seeker finally found her.

Just before lunch, Olive went to her locker to get the sandwich that she'd planned to eat in the basement stairwell. But the moment she tugged the locker door open, a small, folded paper emblazoned with the name *OLIVE* fluttered out onto her shoes.

Panic hit Olive like a semi truck. She whirled around, scanning the busy hallway for any traces of Annabelle— the whispering hem of a long skirt, or the flash of dark hair around a corner. There was no sign of her.

Shakily, Olive bent down and picked up the note. Her enemy had been inside the school again. She had watched Olive go to her locker, had memorized the number, and had come back to slip this message through the closed door. But as Olive unfolded the note, she realized that it was not from the enemy she had expected.

Olive, read the note, in small, square print,

Initially I had planned to shoot this message into your house, wrapped around the shaft of an arrow, in the style of medieval messengers who were unable to surmount a castle's barricades, but my grandmother eventually convinced me that this would be a wiser method. In any case, to show that you have received this missive, please attach the enclosed heraldic flag to your sleeve.

With a sigh, Olive picked up the small blue paper flag that had been folded inside the note and taped it to her arm.

We have highly important matters to discuss, the note went on.

I have information to impart that I am sure will interest you. If you agree to this conclave (a conclave is a secret meeting; the term comes from medieval Latin; "clave" means key, and this type of meeting was often held in locked rooms), join me at our usual table for lunch.

Your ally,
Rutherford

Information that would interest her? Olive crushed the note into a small white ball. Rutherford was wrong about that. She wasn't interested in hearing one more word about that amazing international school in Sweden. She shoved the crumpled note into her pocket, grabbed her lunch, and stomped toward the cafeteria.

The moment Olive stepped into the room, Rutherford's head snapped up. He craned in his seat at their empty table, testing the air like a dog who's just heard a sound too faint for any humans to catch it.

Olive pretended to ignore him. She turned to the side, so that Rutherford could get a clear view of the blue paper flag on her sleeve. Then, still feeling Rutherford's eyes on her, she stalked straight back out the lunchroom doors and down the hall to the deserted stairwell, where the wrappings of yesterday's lunch were waiting for her.

On the bus ride home, Olive took a seat next to a stranger, just to make sure that Rutherford couldn't sit beside her there either. The moment that the doors whooshed open at the bottom of Linden Street, she jumped down the steps and broke into a run, her shoes slapping the leaf-strewn pavement. But their slapping wasn't quite loud enough to cover up the sound of Rutherford shouting after her.

"Olive!" he called. "Olive! Halt!"

Olive didn't turn around. A split second later, the sound of two more running feet joined hers.

"Olive!" Rutherford shouted. "I have been attempting to get your attention all week! I have something important to tell you!"

Olive ran faster. Shade thrown by the towering trees rippled around her, whipping airy black stripes over her skin.

"Olive! In the name of our friendship, I ask you to STOP!"

Now Olive whirled around. She halted so suddenly—and Rutherford was moving so quickly—that he smacked straight into her, and the two of them toppled into a neighbor's bulb garden in a tangle of legs and backpacks.

"In the name of our friendship?!" Olive repeated. She jumped to her feet. "Some friendship, when one of the *friends* keeps a huge secret from the other one!"

"Why are you so angry about this?" Rutherford panted, carefully brushing off his green dragon T-shirt before stepping back onto the sidewalk.

"Why didn't you tell me you were going to leave?" Olive countered. "Were you just going to disappear and let me wonder what had happened to you? Why was it *Annabelle* who had to tell me you were keeping something from me? Should I trust *Annabelle* more than I trust *you?*"

"This is exactly what she was trying to do with that note, you realize," said Rutherford rapidly, jiggling back and forth inches from Olive's face. "She was trying to come between us, so you wouldn't let me or my grandmother help you anymore, by persuading you not to trust me."

"Well, that wouldn't have been so easy to do if you hadn't given her such good *material!*" Olive shouted.

Rutherford blinked at her through his smudgy glasses. "You've kept some awfully important things from *me*," he said.

"I didn't—" Olive spluttered. "I mean, how did you—"

"Hello, you two," said a pleasant voice. A soft white hand landed on Olive's shoulder. "Why don't we take this shouting match indoors, where the neighbors can't overhear every word?"

Olive looked up into Mrs. Dewey's tightly smiling face.

"I have a fresh batch of double-chocolate chocolate chip cookies cooling in the kitchen," Mrs. Dewey went on, taking a firm hold of Olive's wrist before she could squirm away. "And this time," she added more quietly, "I insist that *you* come inside and try one."

Something in Mrs. Dewey's voice convinced Olive not to argue. The words *double-chocolate chocolate chip* didn't hurt either.

With the other hand, Mrs. Dewey grabbed her grandson by the arm. "Come along, Rutherford. And keep quiet until we're inside."

Rutherford obeyed the "come along" part of the command, but the "keep quiet" part seemed to have missed his ears entirely.

"I got an A on my history quiz today, Grandma," he announced, pointedly ignoring Olive as Mrs. Dewey hustled the two of them up the sidewalk. "I only got one question wrong. Well, that is, one of my answers was *marked* wrong, even though it was actually correct. The question was, 'What is the name for the time period from approximately 500 to 1500?' and the answer the teacher wanted was 'The Middle Ages,' but of course, the people of that time didn't call it 'The Middle Ages,' they called it 'The Sixth Age,' because they didn't know they were in the *middle* of anything, so I wrote that the most appropriate name for that time period would actually be 'The Sixth Age,' in Augustinian terms." Rutherford paused to take a breath.

"Only one wrong is still very good," said Mrs. Dewey, opening the door and ushering them inside.

"But I *didn't* get it wrong, I was—"

"Come into the kitchen, both of you," said Mrs. Dewey.

The first time Olive had visited Mrs. Dewey's house, she had been much too terrified of Mrs. Dewey herself to take a good look around. All she had gotten was a foggy impression of a place full of plants. Now Olive's mind brushed the fog away and added a thousand vivid details to the greenish background.

Olive's impression hadn't been wrong. Mrs. Dewey's house *was* full of plants. In fact, it looked a bit like a wallpapered greenhouse with some ruffled, squishy furniture thrown in. Her front hallway and living room and dining room were crowded with shelves and tables and pedestals, all of which were covered with potted plants. Plants with long, trailing tendrils hung from the ceiling. Plants with tiny tufted blossoms basked in the sun on the windowsills. Even the uphol- stered couches were covered with patterns of leaves and flowers.

Mrs. Dewey dragged Olive and Rutherford into the kitchen, where another row of plants in tiny white pots sat in the window above the kitchen sink and the scent of melted chocolate wafted through the air. Hundreds of canisters and bottles and jars, all filled with powders and seeds and flavorings and spices— sort of like the jars beneath Olive's basement, but prettier and more edible—lined the countertops and shelves. A little table, set for three, stood on the spot- less linoleum.

Olive flopped into a chair, folded her arms, and glared intently at the tablecloth. Rutherford plopped into the opposite chair, frowned at Olive for a moment, and then turned his scowl on the tablecloth as well. Mrs. Dewey clicked back and forth in her tiny high heels, pouring milk and arranging cookies. Finally, she took the chair between the two of them, glanced back and forth at their angry faces, and looked curiously down at the tablecloth to see what it had done wrong. Then she sat back in her chair and heaved a sigh.

"So Rutherford told you about the international school," she said.

Olive went on glaring silently at the tabletop.

"He's had a very difficult time making this decision, Olive," Mrs. Dewey went on. Her voice was gentle. "I think he's still not sure that he's doing the right thing. Part of him would like to be with his parents in Europe, but another part of him feels that he should stay here and be your friend and help you." Mrs. Dewey turned to her grandson. "Isn't that right?"

"Approximately," muttered Rutherford.

Olive's and Rutherford's eyes met for a split second before zooming off in different directions.

"We *both* want to help you, Olive," said Mrs. Dewey. "Your problems are awfully large to deal with them all on your own."

Olive felt a lump starting to form in her throat.

"Have a cookie," said Mrs. Dewey, holding the plate under Olive's nose. The scent of warm chocolate wafted right down into Olive's lungs, loosening the lump just a little.

"As you know, I've been keeping an eye on your house," Mrs. Dewey continued, watching Olive take a first bite. "The charm I used keeps any uninvited guests from getting inside. And as far as I can tell, the charm is doing its job. But . . ." Mrs. Dewey let out a ladylike breath through her nose. "I'm afraid that . . . in spite of my best efforts . . . something may have gotten in."

Olive swallowed a half-chewed bit of cookie. "What?" she coughed. "But how?"

Mrs. Dewey passed Olive a napkin. "Well, that's the odd thing. Whatever it is, it didn't break the charm. This means that it either got into the house by some magical, unexpected means—or it was *invited* in."

Olive stared at Mrs. Dewey's soft, round face. But she wasn't seeing Mrs. Dewey at all. Instead, she was seeing her own mother in the front entryway of the old stone house, opening the door, saying, *Come in, please. I could count the number of visitors we've had in this house on one hand . . .*

Olive's fingers went numb. Her half-eaten cookie slipped out of her hand and tumbled onto the flowery tablecloth. "Can you tell who it is?"

Mrs. Dewey nibbled thoughtfully at a cookie. "I'm afraid I can't. I can't say who or what it is, if it's a portrait or a person, or how it got there. All I can say for certain is that there is a malevolent presence in your house."

"Her house always feels like that," said Rutherford.

Mrs. Dewey pursed her little pink lips.

"What can we do?" Olive whispered.

"Have another cookie," said Mrs. Dewey, even though Olive hadn't finished her first one. She gave Olive an encouraging smile. "There isn't much that double-chocolate chocolate chip cookies can't illuminate."

Mrs. Dewey watched as Olive took a bite. The cookie was warm and rich and delicious . . . but underneath the familiar tastes was something rusty and spicy, which didn't taste familiar at all.

"Is there something *special* in these cookies?" Olive asked slowly.

Mrs. Dewey's smile turned knowing with a hint of coy. "I find that after I've eaten a few of these cookies, I can see things a bit more clearly," she said. "Take one more for the walk home, Olive. And tonight, *keep your eyes open.*"

Mrs. Dewey began to gather up the plates and cups. Rutherford sat very still in his chair, avoiding Olive's eyes. Olive wavered to her feet. She couldn't think of what to say to him. So many words were crowding her mind, shoving each other toward the exit, that none of them could get out at all. She managed to whisper "Good-bye," although anyone watching her would have thought she was talking to the tablecloth.

"Good-bye," Rutherford mumbled back.

As she stumbled through Mrs. Dewey's front door, the thought crossed Olive's mind that Rutherford might have been saying *good-bye* for good.

18

THE OLD STONE house was empty and dim. Olive's footsteps thumped through the silence, their echoes ringing off the walls. She slumped up the stairs to the second floor and was about to throw herself face down onto her bed with Hershel when, out of the corner of her eye, she spotted a familiar furry form.

Horatio sat on the carpet at the far end of the hall way, staring up at a painting on the wall. He gave a little jerk as Olive approached.

"Olive," he said, getting up and moving toward her. "You're home. I didn't realize how late it had gotten."

Olive sank down against the wall. She reached out to stroke Horatio's head, but she'd barely felt the cool strands of fur against her fingers before Horatio ducked out of reach.

"You're still angry with me about the paints, aren't you?" she asked.

"Angry?" Horatio repeated. "No, Olive, I'm not angry with you." But the cat continued to back away from her, edging slowly toward the stairs.

"It seems like you've been avoiding me," Olive persisted. "I thought maybe we could go exploring together, or we—"

"I have more important things to do at present, Olive, than playing with children." Horatio turned away. "Now, if you'll excuse me, I will be going outside."

"Are you making sure no one gets into the tunnel again?" Olive asked, following Horatio to the head of the staircase. "You and Harvey filled in the hole, right?"

Horatio hesitated. He descended a few steps before looking back at Olive. "Yes, of course," he said at last. "No one has tried to reach the tunnel again, as far as we can tell. But it is wise to be cautious."

"'The price of safety is eternal vigilance,'" Olive quoted with a little smile. Horatio looked blank. "That's what Leopold always says," she added.

"Ah. Leopold. Yes." Horatio gave her a long look before bounding down the rest of the stairs into the hall below. The last Olive saw of him was a glint of daylight from the front windows glancing off of his sleek orange fur.

She gazed along the hall, back to the spot where Horatio had sat. He'd been staring up at the painting of the craggy hill. Olive wandered toward the painting. She stood in front of it for quite a while, wondering what Horatio had seen that had held his interest so tightly, but today, there was no hint of smoke, no twirling leaves. Looking at that little stone church, no one would ever guess that it held Olive's secret. No one would know why this painting suddenly made Olive shiver from head to toe. Olive herself wasn't quite sure.

That night, after dinner in the old stone house, Mr. Dunwoody suggested that they all play a round of Forty-two, the more complicated version of Twenty-one that Alec and Alice had invented back in their college days.

"It is Friday night, after all," he said, smiling around the dinner table. "I think it calls for something special."

"Not Forty-two," moaned Olive.

Mrs. Dunwoody's face lit up. "Why don't we go to the grocery store?" she suggested.

Olive sank down into her chair. The Dunwoodys had invented another math game for the grocery store, informally known as Total Plus Tax, in which each family member took part of the shopping list, estimated the exact total cost of the items (including tax, if any), and split up, trying to shop so that their purchases added up to that estimate. Whoever came closest was the winner. Olive didn't know what reward the winner got, exactly, because she'd never won, but she guessed that it was something she could live without.

"Not grocery shopping," she moaned.

After some more suggesting and discussing and moaning, Mr. Dunwoody proposed that they all go for a walk. Olive was out of objections at this point. Besides, the sun was just going down, and the sky that could be glimpsed through the windows was a streaked canvas of pale gold and fiery red and dark, encroaching purple. It might be nice to walk under it.

The few scattered streetlights had just flickered on as the Dunwoodys climbed down from their front porch. The very last rays of the sun lingered on Linden Street's tallest houses, making their rooftops shine like bronze until the darkness snuffed them, one by one.

Leaves stirred by an evening breeze clicked softly to the pavement as they walked. Olive kicked a crackling pile beneath Mr. Fergus's big maple tree and listened to them whisper back to the ground before being crunched under her parents' feet. Mrs. Dunwoody counted them before they landed. "Forty-seven," she murmured to Mr. Dunwoody.

They wound their way slowly up and down the block, passing the Butlers' glowing windows and catching a trail of piano music that trickled out of Mr. Hanniman's living room. Mrs. Dewey's cozy house was lit up inside. Olive wondered whether she and Rutherford were having another botany lesson, or if they were washing the dinner dishes and talking about medieval battle tactics, or if Rutherford was in his room, putting stacks of dragon T-shirts and an army of carefully wrapped figurines into a suitcase. A twinge of pain shot through her heart.

The last hint of sunset had vanished by the time they passed Mrs. Nivens's empty house. Olive shuddered, gazing at those black, empty windows, and slowed her steps until her parents caught up with her.

"Strange about Mrs. Nivens, isn't it?" said Mr. Dunwoody, nodding at the tall gray house.

"Strange and sad," said Mrs. Dunwoody.

"Yes," whispered Olive.

Mr. and Mrs. Dunwoody had been holding hands, but now they let go of each other to wrap their arms around Olive's shoulders. Wedged right between them, Olive felt safer and warmer. The heap of worry even began to lighten a little. But as they passed the shriveling lilac hedge, the full height of the old stone house loomed over them. Olive looked up at those dark, empty windows and felt the house looking down at her in return, beckoning her, *daring* her to come back inside. And she had nowhere else to go. Perhaps she was only imagining it, but it seemed as though one last beam of sunset—a beam that should already have slipped behind the horizon—fell across the front steps, leading like a glowing carpet to the front door.

With a nervous, bumpy feeling in her stomach, Olive followed her parents up the creaking porch steps and back inside the old stone house.

K *EEP YOUR EYES OPEN.*
Olive repeated Mrs. Dewey's instructions to herself as she lay in bed, staring up at the ceiling. The shadows of leafy branches danced and skittered across the plaster. What was the "malevolent presence" Mrs. Dewey had detected? Was it Ms. Teedlebaum? Was it Annabelle herself? Was it someone—or something—else? And how would simply keeping her eyes open let her uncover the truth?

Olive turned these questions over and over in her mind until they started to dissolve, crumbling apart like a cookie, or like a torn-up sheet of paper . . .

. . . And suddenly her eyelids were snapping open and she was staring up into the darkness, feeling as though she had been dropped into her bed from a hundred feet above.

How had she let herself fall asleep?

Bolting upright, she turned toward the alarm clock. It was already after 3:00 a.m. Whatever had been making noises in the hallway might have passed by long ago.

Olive glanced from the alarm clock to the door, which she had left open just an inch. Instead of a strip of hallway lit by the pale gray glow of the moon, a wavering band of blue light slipped through the gap in the door. As Olive stared, the light seemed to brighten, stretching across her floor all the way to the side of her bed. It touched the rumpled blankets, poking and prodding at Olive's legs.

As quietly as she could, Olive climbed out of bed and let the beam of light lead her to the door. The hallway was empty. The lights weren't on; no one carrying a magical lantern or a strange, blue-bulbed flashlight was passing by. And yet, a ribbon of blue light filled the corridor, unrolling itself like a carpet just wide enough for one person to walk on. It led from Olive's bedroom door, past the paintings of Linden Street and the moonlit forest, and down into the darkness of the lower floor.

Olive blinked. She rubbed her eyes and looked again and blinked some more. The carpet of light didn't go away. If anything, it seemed to grow brighter, becoming a pearly blue river of light that lapped at Olive's toes.

Mrs. Dewey's words—*There isn't much that double-chocolate chocolate chip cookies can't illuminate*—floated through Olive's memory. There was something here for her to find, and this light was leading the way. She edged out into the hall. The ribbon of light tugged her forward, its beams falling from nowhere, leaving everything outside its stream in darkness. Olive waded in the light, following its path along the corridor and down the stairs.

In the entryway, the carpet of light zagged to the left, leading along the hall toward the kitchen. Olive passed the hollow doorways of the parlor and the dining room. The glowing pathway guided her through the darkness, turning again once it reached the kitchen and trickling beneath the basement door.

Great, muttered Olive's brain. *It would send me down there.*

With a fortifying breath, she turned the knob of the basement door.

The carpet of light sliced through the blackness without lessening it. The basement's dark, hidden corners remained dark and hidden as Olive edged down the chilly wooden steps, shifting her weight from board to board as slowly as she could.

The carpet of light stopped at the foot of the stairs. Olive reached the icy basement floor and paused, looking around, longing to reach for the light chain. The air was as black as spilled ink. Fragments of moonlight from the open doorway above only seemed to outline the darkness. She listened. The basement appeared to be empty, but from somewhere—somewhere distant and enclosed, somewhere that seemed to be beneath her feet—Olive caught the sound of voices.

Could her art teacher possibly be hiding underneath her house? Or could a living portrait with honey-colored eyes and soft, dark hair be lurking just a few steps away? And how odd had Olive's life become that these two possibilities seemed equally likely?

She tiptoed across the cold stone floor to Leopold's corner, following the sound. Behind her, the ribbon of blue light wavered slightly. A cold draft of air told her what she had already guessed: The trapdoor was standing open.

"She's been up there," said a voice—a low, whispering voice—from far beneath.

Olive inched along the wall beside the open trapdoor, trying not to think of the spiders and webs and sucked-dry bodies of bugs that might be scattered there, and lay down on the chilly basement floor, bringing her ears as close to the hole as she dared.

The voice that spoke next was deep and gravelly: Leopold. "I simply can't believe that she would—"

"You *can't* believe it? After the way she manipulated

you?" the other, whispering voice interrupted. Now Olive recognized it. It was Horatio's. "Is your memory that short?"

They must be near the foot of the ladder under the trapdoor, Olive realized. Their voices were close by, but muted and echoing, like sounds made inside of a deep well. She craned over the hole.

A third voice was speaking. At first, Olive couldn't make out what it said, but then she caught the words *double agent* spoken in a crisp British accent. So Harvey was down there too.

She's been up there. Did Horatio mean Annabelle? *She* had certainly manipulated Leopold—and Horatio, and Harvey—in her time. But *double agent?* There was nothing *double* about Annabelle. Her agenda was perfectly clear. Could he mean Ms. Teedlebaum? No, that wouldn't make sense . . . Ms. Teedlebaum had never even seen the cats, as far as Olive knew. But who else could they be talking about?

Horatio's irritated whisper trailed up through the hole again. ". . . What would it take to make you believe . . ."

"Simply don't see why she would—" Leopold's voice ended with another incomprehensible mutter.

"I can assure you that she *has* been up there." Harvey was speaking again. "I observed her myself, from my base of operations. Much as it saddens me to think that one of our own has become a traitor to the cause, it would not be the first time . . ."

"No," said Leopold's voice, soft but clear. "No."

The word echoed in Olive's head. *No.*

"You refuse to believe us?" said Horatio's voice. "I'll show you."

There was some softer, lower mumbling. The ladder gave a faint creak. Olive squirmed away from the trapdoor and pressed herself tight against the basement wall, futilely attempting not to think about the things with many legs that might be crawling from the stones into her hair. She held her breath and kept still.

Horatio and Leopold climbed one after the other through the open trapdoor. Neither one seemed to notice the carpet of pale blue light still glowing on the staircase. Olive pushed her shoulder blades against the gravestones of the wall, trying not to move, not even to blink. The two cats padded silently across the basement floor toward the stairs. Then Horatio halted. He turned to stare into the shadows, right where Olive was sitting. Leopold's eyes swiveled in the same direction. Olive held as still as she had ever held in her life. She pretended that her skin had turned to plastic and that she couldn't feel the cold against her back, or the itchy grittiness under her palms, or the air that was starting to burn in her lungs. She stared straight back at the cats.

"Does she think that we can't see her?" Leopold asked Horatio.

"That would be my guess," said Horatio dryly. "Take a breath, Olive. You look like you're about to give yourself brain damage."

Olive took a gulp of air.

"Ordinarily, I would reprimand you for eavesdropping," Horatio went on, "but as it happens, this is rather convenient. Come with us, Olive. I have something to show both of you."

Wavering to her feet, Olive followed the two cats up the rickety staircase. Neither of them paid any notice to the ribbon of light, sometimes trotting on its blue path, sometimes darting off of it, as though they didn't see it at all—and of course, Olive realized, this was because they *couldn't* see it. Horatio led the way up the stairs, now and then glancing back to check on the other two. Leopold stayed behind him, right in front of Olive, but he did not turn around. He didn't speak either.

"What about Harvey?" Olive asked as they stepped through the basement door. "Isn't he coming?"

"*Harvey* does not require convincing," said Horatio, with a short, hard glance at Leopold.

The pathway of light crossed the kitchen and trailed into the hall, just as it had when Olive followed it to the basement. Olive veered away from the path and dug a flashlight from the kitchen drawers, just in case. "You two can see in the dark, but I need some help," she explained.

Horatio gave an irritated huff before turning and leading the way forward.

They continued along the glowing ribbon of light. Horatio climbed the stairs and turned to the right, trotting past Olive's bedroom. Olive noticed that the light no longer ended at her bedroom door. Instead, it continued down the hall, lengthening as she tiptoed along its width, almost as though it too, were following Horatio's silent footsteps.

Moving faster now, Horatio and the ribbon of light raced past the lavender bedroom and the blue bedroom, making for the pink room. A prickly sense of foreboding moved from the tips of Olive's fingers up the length of her arms.

"Are we going into the attic?" she asked. But the cats didn't answer.

By the time she reached the painting of the ancient city, the light was already there, glowing in the surface of the canvas. Neither cat offered her his tail. Olive fumbled to put on the spectacles as Horatio gave Leopold a commanding nod, and the black cat leaped through the frame.

"After you, Olive," Horatio murmured. "I insist."

Olive plunged through the canvas with Horatio pressed watchfully against her leg, tripping over the bottom of the frame and almost falling face-first through the attic door. The cat raced up the steps into the shadows.

But for the glowing blue ribbon leading her up the stairs, the darkness in the attic was smothering. What little moonlight slipped through the small round window was all that kept the walls from disappearing into solid blackness. Olive flicked on the flashlight, slashing its beam across the room. She gave a little jump when she spotted another light shining back at her, but this turned out to be a reflection from the cluster of mirrors. Still, if Olive's heart had been beating at high speed before, now it kicked up to a drum roll.

Both cats had darted away into the shadows. Olive hesitated at the top of the stairs, testing the darkness with the flashlight while the rivulet of magical blue light lapped at her bare feet. For a moment, the light seemed to condense, making itself brighter . . . and then it reached out one radiant blue beam that unrolled across the attic floor like a skein of silk.

Olive followed the path of light as it wound between the attic's usual oddities—the miniature cannon, the skeletal hat racks—until it stopped beneath the ghostly shape of the cloth-draped easel. There, the light gave a final flare before sinking slowly into darkness.

The flashlight wavered in Olive's hand. Her racing heart jerked to a halt.

Wait a minute . . .

The cloth that covered the painting had been moved. Olive was sure of it. Where before it had hung in even ripples all the way to the floor, now it looked slightly lopsided, as though someone had tossed it hurriedly into place. She ventured closer to the easel. Two paintbrushes, their bristles still damp, stuck out from behind the cloth, on the easel's shelf. A smudge of brown paint stained the fabric—a smudge that Olive was positive hadn't been there before.

Horatio and Leopold slipped out of the darkness and seated themselves in front of the easel.

"Olive," Horatio commanded, "uncover the painting."

Olive gripped the flashlight in her left fist. Her right hand shook as she reached out for the drop cloth. Then, with one quick motion, as though she were pulling off an especially large and bloody bandage, Olive ripped the cloth aside.

Aldous McMartin stared back at her from the easel.

Olive stopped breathing.

It was easy to recognize him. His face had burned itself into her brain when she'd found his photograph in the lavender room's dresser months ago. Now, out of the corner of her eye, she spotted that very same photograph sitting on the easel's shelf, removed from

its old-fashioned folder and propped amid a collection of brushes and fresh splatters of paint.

With or without the photograph, she would have known that face: that rigid, carved-looking face, with its jutting cheekbones and square jaw and eyes that burned like fires in two deep, dark pits. A pair of arms, now complete, ran down to the long, bony hands that Olive had wrestled for the spellbook. The top of his head was missing, so he had no hair, and one of his shoulders was only a murky outline, but it was clear that this portrait was only a few hours—perhaps less—from completion. And, as Olive stood staring, unable to breathe, the portrait shifted. Aldous McMartin's burning eyes locked with hers. His fingers, long and bony, twitched on the pages of the open scrapbook. And then he started to smile.

Olive yanked the spectacles off of her face with such force that their ribbon gouged into her neck. She nearly lost her grip on the flashlight, fumbling it so that its beam raced back and forth across the portrait, gleaming on the glossy streaks of fresh paint. Aldous's eyes seemed to glimmer, as though he was watching her, even now.

"You see, Leopold?" said Horatio's voice from the darkness behind her. "I told you that she was working against us."

20

OLIVE WHIRLED AROUND. Shakily, she aimed the flashlight at the cats. Its beam flared in Leopold's bright green eyes, like a match touching a wick. Horatio dodged the light. He edged to one side, staring hard at Olive as he spoke.

"This is what she's been up to," he said softly. "Didn't I tell you, Leopold? Do you believe me now?"

Leopold's eyes flickered, but he didn't speak.

"*What?*" gasped Olive, whose mind was racing like a mixer in a bowl full of batter, spattering droplets everywhere.

"It was *you* who dug the hole in the backyard, to get the paint-making materials without us knowing," said Horatio.

"No it wasn't!" Olive argued.

But Horatio went on, circling her in the shadows. "It was *you* who reassembled the instructions and took the jars."

"Well—yes, but—"

"It was *you* who mixed the paints. Harvey saw you."

Nothing but air came out of Olive's mouth now. She turned, trying to catch Horatio in the flashlight's beam, but he slipped out of its path again. "I—" she stammered. "But I—I didn't—"

"That's why Harvey remained in the basement, guarding the lower room," said Horatio. "*He* didn't need any more proof of what you'd done."

Leopold shifted uncomfortably. His eyes remained fixed on Olive.

"Leopold," Olive began, "you can search my room if you want to. I don't have the paints or the instructions for making them anymore. I told Horatio to take them away, because I'm never going to use them again, and—"

"*Told* me to take them away?" repeated Horatio. "I *found* them in your room only yesterday. I proceeded to destroy them before you could use them for your dangerous purposes."

Olive's mouth fell open. "Horatio! That's not true! I swear, Leopold," Olive pleaded. "I'm not the one who—"

"Do you deny that you used Aldous's paints to create a portrait?" Leopold demanded, in a voice that was even lower and gruffer than usual.

"No—but I—I just— Honestly, I didn't do *this* one, I was just trying—"

"She was trying to bring Aldous back," said Horatio's voice. Olive slashed at the darkness with the flashlight again, but Horatio remained invisible. "Now she needs him to teach her what she can't master on her own. She wants just what Lucinda Nivens once wanted, just what Annabelle herself once wanted. Didn't she prove as much with the spellbook? She wants to be his apprentice. She wants his power."

"I DO NOT!" Olive exclaimed. "I don't want to be like him! *I didn't do this!*"

Horatio slunk to the edge of the light, standing just over Leopold's shoulder. "She's a danger to all of us," he murmured in Leopold's ear. Horatio stepped forward, nudging Leopold closer to Olive. "Perhaps we should put her into the painting with her master."

Olive took an involuntary step backward and felt her shoulder bump the canvas. She jerked her arm away.

The cats crept closer.

"First, you must give us the spectacles, Olive," Horatio continued. "You are obviously *not* to be trusted."

Olive gulped. The flashlight wavered in her hand, sending a flickering glow over the two cats. Horatio ducked out of the beam once again. "No," Olive said, her voice shaking. "And don't come any closer. I'll scream. My parents will hear."

"They might hear you, but they won't be able to reach you," said Horatio, gliding nearer.

Olive trained the flashlight on his face. Horatio's green eyes narrowed. He stopped moving. In the split second before he turned away, Olive noticed something funny about the shade of his eyes, which weren't quite as bright as they used to be. And his fur . . .

"Horatio," she whispered. "What is *wrong* with you?"

The cat whirled away. "Leopold," he snapped, darting back out of the light, "you and Harvey must remain on continual watch over the subbasement. That way we can ensure that she can't steal any more of the jars. I will take care of this portrait myself."

Leopold gave the tiniest of nods.

"But—then—who will be watching the rest of the house?" asked Olive.

"Who needs to?" Horatio shot back. "We know just where the problem is. It's wherever *you* are."

Olive turned to Leopold, pleading. "Leopold, I swear—you have to believe me—I—"

"*Leopold.*" Horatio cut her off. "Hasn't this girl deceived you enough times for you to learn your lesson? Downstairs. *Now.*"

Leopold hesitated, looking from Horatio to Olive. After another moment, Leopold dragged his eyes away from Olive's face and trudged slowly toward the attic steps. His inky fur was swallowed by the darkness.

With a last hard look at Olive, Horatio backed across the floor, turned, and disappeared silently down the staircase after Leopold.

Olive stood alone in the attic.

In spite of the chilly air, she felt feverish. Her palms were sweating. Her heart thundered. Inside of her head, a flock of questions whirled and dived.

Whatever Horatio had said, *she* knew she hadn't painted Aldous's portrait. All other considerations aside, she simply wasn't a good enough painter. And this meant that someone *else* had painted it.

But who?

Annabelle? She wasn't a painter, as far as Olive knew. Besides, how would Annabelle have gotten into the attic without the spectacles or one of the cats? Ms. Teedlebaum? But she couldn't have gotten into the attic either—and how would she have known where to find the ingredients, let alone concoct the paints? Olive chewed the inside of her cheek, trying to think. Could the bony hands have painted the rest of their body themselves? Olive had no idea, but it seemed pretty unlikely. Horatio was acting so strange . . . Might he have been the painter? Olive tried to picture Horatio holding a brush in one of his furry paws. The image would have made her laugh if she hadn't been so terrified.

Horatio. Olive's vision blurred. She blinked back

the tears, but not before one slid down her chin and soaked into the collar of her pajamas.

What had happened to Horatio? Why had he turned against her—and gotten Leopold and Harvey to desert her as well? Did he truly believe what he told them—that Olive was trying to serve the McMartins? No, Olive reasoned. He *couldn't* believe that. He was the one who knew about her failed painting of Morton's parents; he was the one she had asked to take away the paints and dispose of them for good.

So why had he *lied* about her? The Horatio she knew might have been prickly at times, but he was honest. And, in spite of that prickly exterior, Olive had come to believe that Horatio cared for her, deep down in his centuries-old heart.

This Horatio hardly seemed like the cat she knew at all. *This* Horatio, with his dull eyes, and his cold, hard expression, and his slick, not-quite-soft-enough fur . . .

He looked like *paint*.

A breath of dusty attic air caught in Olive's lungs. The flashlight shook in her hands, sending its jumpy beam over the mountains of clutter.

Her mind flashed through its images of Horatio— the way his fur had flared in the sunlight on her parents' bed, and how warm and soft it had felt under her fingertips; the cool feeling of his ears as he edged away from her in the upstairs hall, the way the light glanced off of him instead of making each orange strand of hair glow—and a sense of certainty began to fill her, like cement pouring into a mold. It made her feel indestructible. And heavy. And ready for whatever might come next.

With a deep, angry breath, Olive turned around and faced the easel. Aldous McMartin gazed back at her. Every nerve in Olive's body wanted to pick up the painting and smash it over the old hat rack, and then to kick its broken frame across the attic, and then perhaps to wad the canvas up and see if the small, battered cannon still worked well enough to launch a crumpled painting through the night air. But Olive stopped herself.

Whoever had been painting the portrait would be back to finish it. And waiting—as difficult as it would be—was probably the only way for Olive to uncover the identity of its painter. Olive would have wagered her whole piggybank that the painted Horatio and the painted Aldous had more than their paint in common.

But she wasn't going to let the painter foil her again. Olive snatched the black-and-white photograph off of the easel's shelf, holding it between the very tips of her fingers, like something that might give her a rash. Without meeting Aldous's green-gold eyes, she covered the horrible portrait with its cloth.

The moonlight falling through the small round window seemed to brighten as Olive hurried across the room, tucking the flashlight under her arm and using both hands to push at the window frame. The swollen wood gave a low, angry groan. Olive froze for a moment, listening, but there was no other sound— nothing but the night wind whispering through the trees.

Leaning through the open window, Olive tore Aldous's photograph to pieces. Then she tore the pieces into even tinier pieces, until there was nothing left that was large enough to tear. She tossed the pieces into the air. A breeze caught them, the fragments scattering and spinning until they were whirled away into the darkness.

Then Olive put the spectacles on and climbed back down the stairs, out of the attic.

A FTER WHAT HAPPENED in the attic that night,
Olive was sure she wouldn't be able to sleep. She
lay down in her bed and rolled herself up in the covers
like silverware inside a napkin, and waited for sleep *not*
to come. But then, suddenly, she was opening her eyes
and her bedroom was sparkling with morning sun and
the smell of breakfast was drifting up from downstairs.
She was sure she would never be able to eat again
either, but as it turned out, she managed to put away
four muffins and a massive glass of orange juice before
she even realized that she was hungry. And maybe it
was the sleep, or maybe it was the fortification of muffins, but Olive began to feel more and more *steely* as the
morning went on.

Once she had finished helping dry the breakfast

dishes and Mr. and Mrs. Dunwoody were happily settled at the table with fresh coffee and giant stacks of quizzes to correct, Olive hurried back up the stairs, put on the spectacles, and climbed into the painting of Linden Street.

She tore up the misty hill, toward a small white blotch on Morton's porch. As she raced closer, the blotch clarified into Morton himself. He was seated on the floor with the folds of his white nightshirt pooled around him, sorting through the pieces of the gigantic jigsaw puzzle Olive had brought.

"Morton!" she gasped. "Morton, I need to talk to you."

"Found another edge piece," said Morton, still sorting through the puzzle box. He glanced at her out of the corner of his eyes. "Is it about that other *boy* again?"

"No," said Olive emphatically. "It's not about . . . him." Olive dropped onto the porch steps, pressing her hand to the cramp in her side, where some muffins seemed to be reassembling themselves. "It's about this house. And the McMartins. And Horatio. And it's *important*."

Morton dropped his handful of puzzle pieces. "Important?" he repeated doubtfully.

"Yes." Olive leaned forward, bringing her face close to Morton's. "Something terrible has happened to Horatio. Somehow . . . he's been turned into paint."

Morton frowned. "How?"

"That's part of the problem. I don't *know* how. Maybe he got stuck in Elsewhere too long, just like you, and he—"

But Morton was already shaking his head. His tufts of white hair fluttered in agreement. "The cats stayed here with me lots of times. Like the night when Lucinda was . . ." He trailed off, leaving the sentence unfinished. "They stayed for a long time. And they didn't change." He looked back at Olive, and his face took on an explain-y, teacher-y expression. "They're not really *alive,* you know."

"I know," said Olive, with a shade of irritation.

"Look," Morton went on, lifting a puzzle piece and waving it in front of Olive's nose. "Not alive," he said slowly. "Not turning into paint. And the papers you brought for me to put together. They weren't alive. They didn't turn into paint."

"Right," said Olive. "So . . . he can't be the same Horatio." There was a panicky catch in her chest as she realized what else this would mean. The real Horatio—the one she knew and trusted and *needed*—was gone. "But where did the real one go?"

"Well," drawled Morton, still sounding like he was talking to a kindergartener and enjoying it very much, "where's the last place you saw him acting like the normal Horatio?"

Mr. and Mrs. Dunwoody often used this sort of questioning with Olive. *Well, where's the last place you saw your retainer? Did you have it in your mouth when you woke up? Was it there before you went to bed? How did it end up behind the frozen peas?* Now her brain clicked backward through its collection of Horatio memories: His strange behavior in the attic last night, as he tried to avoid the flashlight's beam. His silhouette gliding past Olive's bedroom door after she'd been woken by the recurrent bumps and creaks. His green eyes tilting up toward the painting of the craggy hill, where she'd surprised him one afternoon. His cold claw, stuck to the cuff of her blue jeans as she fell back through the frame around the *very same painting . . .*

Olive sucked in a breath. "I'm going to come back here tonight," she said slowly. "I think from inside this frame I might be able to see what I've been missing." She turned back to Morton. "And, if you wouldn't mind—I'd like your help."

Morton's smile threatened to reach all the way to his ears.

Never in her life had Olive been more impatient for a Saturday to end. She and Mr. Dunwoody raked the backyard, where a thick quilt of maple leaves was already smothering the neatly refilled hole behind the garden. She decorated three rocks with fingernail polish. She even got all of her homework done, with an entire half of the weekend left to go. And still, the evening moved about as quickly as a snail stuck to a wad of chewed bubble gum. After dinner and a seemingly endless game of Forty-two, Olive said good night to her parents and charged up the stairs to her bedroom, where she changed into a black T-shirt and a pair of dark flannel pajama pants. Then she lay down in bed with a book to wait.

After what felt like hours, she heard her parents' footsteps creaking up the staircase. Their bedroom door clicked shut. Olive listened to the roar of blood pounding through her body as several more minutes ticked by. Then, just when she was about to slide out of bed, there was a tiny squeak from her own bedroom door.

Olive froze. A slit of moonlight, no wider than a finger, fell across her bed. Olive lay perfectly still, pretending to be asleep. The slit of moonlight disappeared. A minute later, she heard a soft creak somewhere in the distance. When the house had sunk back into silence, she slipped into the hallway, closed her bedroom door behind her, and dove into the painting of Linden Street.

This time, Morton was waiting for her. When Olive landed with a *flump* on the dewy ground, his round head popped up just a few yards away, the tufts of his pale hair mingling with the long green grass.

"Are you all right?" he asked.

"Fine," whispered Olive. She turned back to peer through the picture frame, but whatever had made the creaking sounds had already disappeared again.

"I wasn't sure when you'd be back, so I just decided to wait here," he told her.

"Thanks." Olive knelt next to Morton in the grass, sending up a swirl of mist that clung stubbornly around her.

"So, what are we watching for?" asked Morton.

Olive hopped up again and beckoned Morton to the picture frame. He stood on his toes to look over its edge. "See how you can look all the way down the hall from here?" Olive asked. Morton nodded. "I think something funny has been going on with that painting—that very last one, down there by the door to the pink room." She pointed. Morton craned to follow her finger. "But I can't see that picture from the door of my own room." Olive sighed, blinking through the frame. "I just hope whatever it is happens again before I have to get back out of here."

For a while, they both stood at the picture frame, gazing over its edge. The hallway was black and still. Even the beams of moonlight on the carpet were motionless. After several silent minutes of watching, they decided to play Twenty Questions, but Morton was jumpy and distracted, and Olive kept seeing imaginary intruders darting down the hallway from the corner of her eye. Olive's toes were just starting to feel prickly and numb and Morton was saying "You already *asked* if it was bigger than a breadbox" for the fifth or sixth time, when, at the far end of the hall, a shadow shifted.

"Look!" whispered Olive. She and Morton huddled below the frame, letting just their eyes peep over its corners.

From the darkness of the pink bedroom, a smaller blot of darkness emerged. It stepped into the hall, where the moonlight from the house's front windows snipped and stretched its shadow. And casting that long black shadow was a cat.

"Is that Horatio?" breathed Morton.

"Sort of," Olive breathed back.

Behind Horatio glided another blot of darkness. This one was tall and thin, and it cast a shadow so long that it reached almost to the frame where Olive and Morton were crouching. Olive squinted at it, trying to get a closer look without letting herself be seen. The shadow moved along the hall, passing briefly through a blue beam of moonlight. In that instant, Olive made out the tall, lean shape of a man's body a man with long, wavy hair and ragged clothes; a man with features that looked as though they could have been carved out of wood. The man was carrying two bags. One bag was small, and had short handles that looped over his left arm. The other was a large cloth sack, kind of like a pillowcase with a drawstring. And something inside of the sack was *moving*.

The sack made a muffled whimpering sound—a sound Olive had heard at least once before. The man gave the sack a sharp shake. The whimpering stopped. He paused before the painting of the craggy hill, and, as Olive stared, barely able to breathe, he reached into the drawstring sack. With his arm still inside it, he climbed into the picture frame, hauling both bags with him.

Horatio sat on the hallway carpet, watching the man disappear. Then the cat got to his feet and trotted along the hall, past the frame of Linden Street, and down the staircase into the darkness.

Morton turned, wide-eyed, to Olive. "Who *is* that? How did he—"

"Morton, I'm not sure what's going on yet, but I need you to follow Horatio. Try to keep him away from the painting that man climbed into. Keep him away from the whole upstairs, if you can. Will you do that?"

Morton nodded.

Olive grabbed him by the hand, and they climbed one after the other through the frame into the upstairs hallway.

"Be careful," Olive whispered.

"*You* be careful," Morton whispered back. Giving her one last anxious glance, he hurried down the stairs.

Olive rushed along the hall, made sure the spectacles' ribbon was secure around her neck, and hoisted herself as soundlessly as she could into the painting of the craggy hill to follow the shadowy man.

AFTER THE DARKNESS of the hallway, the afternoon light inside the painting felt strangely bright. The cloudy gray sky forced Olive to squint. The waves of flowers that surrounded her on all sides now seemed prickly and harsh and threatening. There was something very strange about this place—the way that it changed with every viewing or visit, as though someone were manipulating it. And Olive had a guess about who that *someone* could be.

She took a blinky look around, her mind racing. The young man was nowhere in sight. Still, Olive knew he couldn't be far away, and she did not want to confront him alone. With a last glance around, she set off at a run up the slope toward the little stone church, while the waves of flowers snagged at her pajamas with their jagged stems.

The painting of Morton's parents waited just where she had left it, propped in the church's last pew. Olive grabbed the canvas and carried it back out into the daylight, pausing at the crest of the hill to scan the forest below. There, amidst the trees down the slope to her right, was a ribbon of smoke. Olive tucked the painting under her arm and raced toward the floating trail.

The brambles on the hillside seemed to thicken as she ran through them, their thorny twigs scraping her ankles. She had to stop twice to disentangle her flannel cuff. Then she scurried on even faster, galloping through a hedge of bracken and into the gold-canopied forest. The cold air felt like a saw blade in her throat.

As she neared the cottage, Olive forced her feet to slow down. She dodged from one clump of birch trees to another, staying hidden. Through the papery trunks, she could spot the tiny shack with its steady stream of smoke. Its door stood open, but Olive couldn't hear any sounds coming from inside. Behind a cluster of tree trunks, she propped the painting of Morton's parents on the ground, readjusted the spectacles, and crawled into the canvas.

Mr. and Mrs. Nivens did not look surprised to see her. Of course, they probably wouldn't have looked surprised if she had cartwheeled across their floor, shooting grape jelly from her toes and singing "The Star-Spangled Banner" backward. As Olive got to her feet, panting, they went on smiling glassily. Mrs. Nivens squinted her much-too-large eyes. Mr. Nivens moved one sausagey hand in what might have been a wave or an involuntary nervous spasm. If he *had* nerves, that is.

"Hi," said Olive in a whisper. "I need your help. Will you come with me, please?"

Mr. and Mrs. Nivens went on smiling.

"I'll take that as a yes," said Olive.

She reached for Mrs. Nivens's hand this time. It lay in her grasp like a slick white slug. "Hold on to each other," she commanded. Then she hauled Mr. and Mrs. Nivens through the edge of the canvas, back out into the golden forest.

Once the painted people were upright again, Olive hustled them away from their deserted canvas. She dragged them farther from the cottage, Mr. Nivens marching awkwardly on his kneeless legs, and Mrs. Nivens shuffling along inside of her voluminous skirts, until they had reached the shelter of a gigantic oak tree. The cottage stood in the distance, almost out of sight.

"Okay," Olive whispered. "Now I need you to make some noise."

The painted people smiled at her.

"Noise," Olive repeated. "Sounds. Talking. Anything. *Noise.*"

Mrs. Nivens squinted. Mr. Nivens twitched his furry mustache.

"Make noise!" pleaded Olive. "Arrr! Mmmmmmm! Rarararar! Reeee!"

"Rrrraaarrrr?" said Mr. Nivens.

"MmmmMMMM," said Mrs. Nivens.

"That's it!" Olive exclaimed. "Louder! MMMMM!! RRRRRR!!!"

Mr. and Mrs. Nivens both began talking at once. "MmmmMMMMMmmmm!"

"RAAaaarrrraaaeeeeaahhh . . ."

Olive craned around the tree trunk toward the cottage. The young man's head had appeared in the open door.

"Good!" she whispered, waving her hands like an overzealous orchestra conductor. "Keep going! Mmmmm! Rrrrr!"

"Rrrraaaaaarrrreeeeaaarrrrrr!"

"MmmmmMMMM! MmmmmMMMMMM!!"

The young man stepped out of the shack and stood in front of its open door, craning his head for the source of this strange sound.

"Mmmmm!!!" enthused Mrs. Nivens.

"RRRReeeeeaaarRR!" agreed Mr. Nivens.

The young man headed in their direction.

Olive hunkered low to the ground and sidled around to the other side of the oak tree, leaving the painted people to their noisemaking. The man drew nearer, his bright hazel eyes flicking from side to side. Olive waited until a large gap had formed between him and the cottage. Then, keeping a barrier of trees between her body and the man's line of sight, she bolted toward the clearing.

Olive darted across the ground in a final, panicked burst, and zoomed through the cottage's open door. She peered back out, heart hammering. The young man was still walking slowly away, looking around. She had a little bit of time.

Olive scanned the cluttered room. The tools and utensils and cloths and herbs still hung in clusters on the walls. But where were the two bags the man had been carrying when Olive spotted him in the hall? She dropped to her knees. In the darkness beneath the long, narrow cot pressed into one corner, Olive spotted the leather bag with handles. She dragged it out into the light. Now that she saw it up close, something about the bag looked familiar. She had seen this bag before, she was sure—but it had been part of a jumble of luggage, and it had seemed forgettable and unimportant compared to the more interesting things all around it . . .

The attic. That was where she had seen it. It had

been part of the pile of musty boxes and steamer trunks that had probably gone unused for decades. Now here it was, being used once again. Olive's heart clenched like a fist. *Yes—the young man had been in the attic.* Where *else* had he been? And what else may he have found?

Shaking, Olive unlatched the rusty clasps and looked inside the old leather bag.

It was full of jars. *Her* jars.

Here was the indigo, and the crimson, and the black and white and yellow. And here were smaller, stoppered bottles full of bright, opaque hues, all looking richer and smoother than the versions she had concocted. *Paints.* Olive shook the bottles aside. At the bottom of the bag lay a sheaf of papers, their taped seams reflecting the faint gray daylight that came through the cottage door. Olive's stomach swirled. She grabbed the heavy leather bag, staggering to her feet.

She still had to find the other bag—the one that had moved and whimpered. From somewhere against the cottage's far wall, she heard a weak little thump.

Olive dove into the corner, where there sat a heavy wooden box with a hinged lid. Dropping the leather bag, which hit the floor with a glassy clunk, Olive used both hands to heft the lid open. Inside, half hidden by split firewood, was the drawstring sack. It thrashed and kicked in Olive's arms as she hoisted it.

The bag and its knotted ropes were painted; up close, Olive could see the faint brushstrokes that imitated woven fibers. She pinned the bag to the ground with one knee so that it couldn't leap back into its place in the box, and tried to untie the ropes that held it shut. Not only were the knots tricky to untie, but each time she pulled a painted thread loose, it wove itself into place again. The young man wouldn't be gone for much longer, Olive knew. Desperately, she scanned the tools on the wall. A row of knives hung between a small saw and something that looked like a metal spatula. Still grasping the twisting, jerking bag, which was now emitting a series of impatient grunts, Olive grabbed the smallest knife. She cut through the ropes and tossed them to the ground, where they rapidly rewove and reknotted themselves. Olive yanked the bag open.

Warm orange fur brushed against her skin. Bright green eyes stared up at her above a tightly bound and muzzled mouth.

Being careful not to cut anything that didn't deserve it, Olive slit the cords that held Horatio's paws together and severed the bands of cloth covering his mouth. She dropped the knife, which quickly flew back to its spot on the wall.

"Horatio," she whispered. "I'm so glad to see you. Are you all right?"

"Nothing is all right," hissed the cat. "We need to get out of here."

Before Horatio could protest, Olive scooped up the massive cat in both arms and scuttled clumsily to the doorway. The young man was nowhere in sight. Instead of going back the way she had come, Olive slunk around the cottage in the opposite direction. Then she dashed into the trees with Horatio in tow.

"My hero," said Horatio dryly as he bounced along in Olive's arms. "Might you consider setting me down now? There is a very good reason for more creatures having *four* legs than *two*."

Olive put Horatio down on a thick patch of yellow leaves.

"Thank you," said the cat. His bright eyes surveyed the forest. "This way," he announced, setting off at a brisk trot. Olive scurried after him.

"Horatio, what's going on?" she panted as she ran. "There's the portrait in the attic, and there's another you, but it's just paint, and that homeless man was getting out by using you, I guess, and you—I mean the *other* you—didn't actually get rid of the jars and the paint-making instructions, because that man has them, and the *other* you said I dug the hole in the back-yard, but I didn't, and I don't—"

"Olive," Horatio interrupted as Olive gasped for air, "could you possibly save that ridiculously unclear explanation for a time when we are *not* in immediate danger?" The cat paused, ears and whiskers twitching. He turned slightly to the right before breaking into a run again. "As for what is going on . . . I've had considerable time to ponder that question, as I've spent the last several days tied inside of a potato sack, where entertainment options were a bit limited. Here's what I have gathered: Annabelle *did* dig the hole that led to the tunnel, but she didn't take any of the jars."

"Why not?"

"There would have been no point. She couldn't get the jars to Aldous, inside of Elsewhere. She needed *you* to do that."

Unpleasant memories snagged at Olive like the painted bracken: The locket with Aldous's last portrait, which she had brought straight to Annabelle. The spellbook, which she had unknowingly let lead her around the house, until she had set Annabelle free again.

Olive dug her fingernails into her palms. "She knew just what I would do," she said softly. "She always does."

Horatio glanced up at her, and his eyes were not unkind. "She understands how your mind works, Olive. In some ways, you and Annabelle are very much alike. You're both clever. You're both loyal. You're both *unreasonably obstinate.*" He arched one whiskery eyebrow. "Annabelle guessed that you would bring the papers and paints out of the tunnel, and then the house could guide you exactly where it wanted you. Right here."

Still running, Olive glanced up at the cloudy gray sky. It seemed to grow even darker as she gazed at it— just as the skies had darkened when Olive first visited Elsewhere, when Aldous McMartin was watching over his painted worlds, manipulating them, causing winds to rise and trees to rattle . . .

"He's controlling this place, isn't he?" she asked Horatio, even though she didn't need an answer. She looked over her shoulder at the forest, at the branches rustling in a sudden breeze. He could make the wind blow, and the skies turn black, and one little golden leaf dance through the air. "It's *him,* isn't it?" she whispered.

Horatio stopped, mid-stride, and turned around to stare into her eyes.

"The young man in the shack. He's—" For some reason, Olive couldn't quite say the words. All at once, she realized how Morton and his neighbors felt, barely able to speak the name out loud when its owner might be lurking in the shadows, just out of sight.

Horatio finished her sentence. "Yes, Olive. He is Aldous McMartin."

OLIVE HAD RIDDEN on a Tilt-A-Whirl at a state fair once. Once had been enough. For the rest of the day, she had stumbled around with her head tipped sideways, feeling dizzy and nauseous and trying not to walk into anything. Now, as she chased Horatio's fluffy tail through the bracken, Olive felt as though she were stuck on a Tilt-A-Whirl that might never let her off again.

"I can't believe I didn't figure it out sooner," she moaned. "I thought it must be Annabelle, or my art teacher, and besides, you—the *other* you—said I could trust him, and I trusted *you,* and so I thought . . ."

"I know," said Horatio over his shoulder. "When everyone wants something from you, it can be very difficult to know whom to trust."

Olive let out a short, unhappy laugh. "You know, Annabelle wrote almost the very same thing in a note to me."

Horatio's eyes glinted back at Olive through the gray light. "Did she?" he said. A look of concern landed on his face before flitting briskly away again. "Well—even liars tell the truth now and then." He dodged around a cluster of thorny bushes. His voice trailed back to Olive as she hurried along behind him. "Speaking of the truth," he went on, "I must admit that I didn't know we would find Aldous here either. It was this *place* that I recognized, and therefore tried to avoid . . . until you made a visit compulsory. This is Scotland, Olive. These hills were McMartin land," he explained as they hurried through the shrubbery at the edge of the woods. "When the family manor was burned to the ground by suspicious neighbors, Aldous escaped into the forest. There he hid, waiting and plotting, until he could leave the country once and for all." Horatio glanced up at the flowering hillsides. "As I deliberately stayed away from this particular painting, discovering that Aldous had painted his younger self here, as well as *my* younger self, was nothing but a *delightful* surprise."

"You shouldn't have come in after me," panted Olive.

"Then he would simply have abducted *you* instead.

He would have taken back the spectacles and trapped you here for good. Or disposed of you somehow." Horatio sighed, surveying the hills before darting across the bracken toward the distant picture frame. "They managed to manipulate both of us, and to get exactly what they wanted. By replacing me with that . . . that painted *nitwit*," Horatio growled, "he was able to isolate you, to immobilize me, and to get the paint-making materials. At last, he had the perfect chance to finish the portrait." Horatio gave his head a brisk shake. "The young Aldous may have had some talent, but he's a *schoolboy* compared to the Old Man. And everything that Aldous McMartin learned or mastered or created within his long, cruel lifetime is preserved inside of that portrait." Horatio glanced up at Olive's gloomy face. "But it's all right, Olive," he said, in a voice that was surprisingly gentle. At least, it was surprisingly gentle for Horatio, which was sort of like comparing sandpaper to broken glass. "I'm glad I came in after you. And that you came in after me."

This made Olive want to flop down and hug Horatio until he couldn't breathe, but the cat had already turned away. He nodded toward the picture frame hanging in midair ahead of them. "Once we're out of this painting, Aldous will be stuck, just as he was before. In fact, I'd say we're fortunate: The way everything has happened, we have a chance of getting out of here safely, catching the imposter, and setting every-thing right once again." Horatio resumed his speedy trot. "Believe me, once I get my paws on that inter-loper—"

But before Horatio could say another word, there was a sharp snapping sound, and both Olive and Hora-tio plunged through a layer of bracken into a deep, hidden pit. Olive's brain barely had time to shout, *It's a tiger trap! No, it's a bear trap! No, it's a—* before her feet hit something solid, sending a painful jolt through her spine, and she collapsed in a heap. Several feet above her, the flowering bracken mended itself, forming a net that blocked out all but a few glimmers of gray sky.

"How come we didn't notice this hole before?" Olive gasped, sucking air through her teeth.

"Because it wasn't *here* before," Horatio answered. He had naturally landed on all fours, and now he was pacing back and forth, staring up at the covered mouth of the hole high above. "It was *painted* here." Horatio lifted a paw that bore a smudge of fresh brown paint. "Camouflaged. A trap."

Olive rocked to her feet. Ignoring her bruised back-side, which demanded that she lay down again, prefer-ably on her *front* this time, Olive reached as high as she could up the hole's rocky wall. Her fingertips were a few feet from the opening. Olive jumped, but she still couldn't reach the edge.

"Maybe you could climb up my arms," she told the cat. "Or I could toss you."

Horatio's eyes widened.

Before Olive could make a grab at him, a voice spoke from the lip of the hole.

"I'm afraid that's not going to work."

A shadow passed over the carpet of bracken. A moment later, through a gap in the greenery, the ragged young man from the forest peered down at them. His face twisted with a slow, predatory smile, and all at once, Olive could see that this handsome young man and the terrifying portrait in the attic were not so very different after all.

The man—*Aldous McMartin*, Olive reminded herself—held up a brush and a bottle of paint. Olive's mind flashed back to the glassy clunk of the leather bag hitting the cottage floor. Something equally large and heavy clunked down to the pit of her stomach. "I am not about to let one little girl and one disobedient cat stand in my family's way," he said. Aldous dipped the brush into the bottle. With a few swift flourishes that led from the ground up into the painted air, he made one jagged, forking shape, and then another, and another, until the hole was encircled by small black trees. "Not my best work," he said, "but I'm in a bit of a rush. And speaking of sloppy work, I met your portraits, Olive." Aldous paused to shake his head, smiling. "What a sad pair of specimens. I'm not sure you could have done worse work if you'd tried."

Olive gulped.

Above her head, Aldous took another bottle out of the leather bag and dabbed spots of black and brown and white onto a palette. "You were missing ingredients, you had mixed the paints incorrectly, and on top of that, your technique leaves a great deal to be desired," he said, as patiently as a schoolteacher. "You see?" His brush flicked through the air, leaving a trail of magical paint behind. "All it takes is a line or two to suggest the shape of a plant." Now the brush slashed outward, spinning leaves from the ends of still-damp branches. "What was bare ground minutes ago is now a hedge." Jagged twigs of brown paint entwined in the gray air, branches hooking through branches, woven as tight as a fence. "With a few strokes, the right play of light and color, I could turn flowers into ice. Grass into rock. A bit of bare hillside into an open grave."

Olive had been watching with her mouth open. Now she closed it.

"Horatio," she whispered, her eyes still fixed on Aldous's work, "what is he going to do?"

Horatio was silent.

Aldous's brush hissed through the air like a torch leaving a trail of smoke. Thorns began to sprout from the painted trunks—thorns as big as blades in places, as small and sharp as needles in others. Even the sight of them made Olive wince. When the hole was entirely surrounded by this thicket of knives, Aldous paused and stepped back, surveying his work. "It needs something," he murmured to himself. Then, with a fresh brush and a few rippling strokes, he added red roses, as bright as fresh wounds.

"There," he said. "There's no reason that deadly things shouldn't be beautiful, after all."

Aldous's work *was* beautiful. Olive had to admit it, even if it made her shiver. Peering up through the darkness into Aldous's glittering yellow eyes, Olive thought again of her poor, lumpy portraits of Mr. and Mrs. Nivens, with their flat eyes and lifeless faces. She couldn't hope to compete with Aldous—not with Aldous's own tools. She couldn't defeat him with magic *or* with art. She simply didn't have his talent. The weight of her anger and frustration made it suddenly hard to breathe.

"Now we wait. It shouldn't take long." Aldous smiled again, lowering his paintbrush. "Then I will seal you in. I'll paint a surface so perfectly real, so smoothly blended into the landscape, that no one would ever guess there had been a hole here at all. If, by some impossible odds, anyone should come here to look for you, they will stand right above you, gazing around at the hillsides, never knowing that you are trapped just beneath their feet."

A surge of panic swept through Olive's body, mixing

with her pent-up fury until she was sure that she could have hurled a boulder at Aldous's head—if only she'd had a boulder to hurl. "Why don't you just get it over with?" she demanded.

Aldous's eyebrows went up ever so slightly. "If you were still *alive* when I sealed you in, you might merely suffocate." The eyebrows came back down again as a carnivorous smile uncurled on Aldous's face. "But once you have changed to paint and no longer need to breathe, or eat, or drink, you can remain down there in the darkness forever." The smile widened. "*Forever, Olive.* Can you imagine it? Without even the possibility of death to set you free."

"Aldous," growled Horatio. "Spare the girl."

Aldous paused. His bright yellow-green eyes flickered through the depths of the hole, fixing on Horatio. "What on earth," he began, his voice as low and soft as distant thunder, "would make you think that *you* may ask anything of *me?*" Aldous leaned over the edge of the pit. Between the thorns and the carpet of bracken, Olive watched his face move into clearer view. "You traitor. You *weakling.* Our family already lost our home once. Do you think I would allow that to happen again? I, who have had to live like a pauper on the very land where I should have lived like a king?" Aldous raised the wet paintbrush. "Shall I add some spiders to your cozy little den?" he asked, his voice even softer than before. "A few vipers? A hornets' nest? Or something else to make Olive's last living moments less comfortable?"

Olive gulped, glancing from Aldous's eyes to the hedge of deadly thorns. Horatio didn't move.

Aldous waited. "Speak again, and I will," he murmured, when it was clear that Horatio was not going to answer. "I believe I will let Horatio stay and watch you change into paint, Olive. It might be unpleasant for him. He seems to care about you." Aldous's eyes traveled back to the cat. "Once my family has reclaimed this house and everything in it—which includes your misguided compatriots, Leopold and Harvey"— Aldous's voice coiled around them like the hiss of a snake—"we shall devise some special punishments for *you*, Horatio."

Gathering up the jars and brushes, Aldous turned away from the pit. In a moment, he had vanished. Olive listened to his steps crunching away across the brush.

"What do you think he's doing?" she whispered to Horatio.

"Waiting," he answered.

"Where do you think he's going?"

"Not far."

For a moment, they were both still. Between the bruised ache of her backside and the pounding of her heart, Olive hadn't noticed the fainter discomfort of her feet, or the way that her ankles were beginning to prickle and go numb. Through the lacy shadows from above, she glanced down at her hand. The skin was shiny and streaked.

"Horatio . . ." she whispered.

Horatio's eyes followed hers. "Has it already been so long?" he asked.

"First I watched the hallway with Morton from inside his painting for a long time, and then I came in here . . ."

Even in the dimness at the bottom of the pit, Olive could see Horatio hang his head. "I'm sorry, Olive," he said. "I'm sorry that I couldn't save you."

"*I'm* sorry," said Olive. "It's my fault for using the paints and climbing in here in the first place."

They were quiet once again. After a moment, Olive threw herself at the rocky wall, pawing and kicking, but she couldn't get a foothold. When she managed to scrape a bit of dirt out of place, it only flew back to its own spot, forming the same un-climbable surface. And even if she reached the top, she doubted that she could survive those thorns.

She slumped back down to the ground. The prickling feeling was climbing toward her knees. Her hands felt numb. In the darkness a few inches from her side, Horatio sat as still as a stone.

"Horatio," Olive whispered. "If I'm sort of . . . um . . . like Annabelle used to be, does that mean that you and Annabelle . . . that you were friends?" She swallowed. "I mean . . . did you care about *her?*"

She heard Horatio let out a little breath. "Well, Olive," he said, "that's where you two are quite different."

They were silent for another moment.

"Horatio," Olive choked, "if you *do* eventually get out of here, would you tell everybody—I mean my parents and Morton and Leopold and Harvey and Rutherford—"

"Yes, Olive," Horatio prompted. "Everybody."

"Would you tell them that I—"

"Freeze!"

Olive and Horatio obeyed.

"Agent Olive! Agent Orange!" shouted a voice with a faint British accent. "Don't move! We've got you covered!"

T WO CATS—ONE LARGE and black, one small and splotchily colored—and one mussy-haired boy in dragon pajamas peered over the thorny edge of the hole, high above.

At first Olive was sure she was dreaming; her own imagination was bringing her friends to save her in the nick of time. Then she noticed that Rutherford was holding two small pistols. A third pistol was clamped between Leopold's teeth. A fourth was strapped to a miniature holster that was belted across Harvey's chest. Even Olive's imagination would not have done *that*.

As Olive stared, Rutherford aimed both his pistols at the mass of thorns. She gritted her teeth and prepared for a bang. Instead, all she heard was a soft hiss.

She looked up. "Water pistols?"

Rutherford glanced down at her, still spraying. "Filled with paint thinner," he explained. "And a mixture of my grandmother's herbs."

Harvey leaped onto the dripping stems, smearing them wildly with both paws. "Take that!" he shouted. "And that! Don't try to tangle with Agent 1-800!" The fresh paint, coated with sparkling liquid, rapidly began to dissolve, sending rivulets of melting black and red down the side of the pit toward Olive's toes.

"Grab my hands!" said Rutherford, leaning over the cleared space and reaching into the hole. Olive grabbed. Before Rutherford could begin to pull, Horatio clambered up the ladder made by their bodies and perched on the hole's edge.

"Come on, Olive," he urged. "Climb!"

Hanging on to Rutherford's hands, Olive struggled up the wall, her numb feet slipping in the streams of paint. Leopold's paw caught the fabric of her shoulder, Harvey's teeth closed around a hank of her hair, and suddenly, Olive was crawling out of the pit, knocking Rutherford backward and blinking in the gray daylight.

"Arm yourself, miss," Leopold commanded, dropping a spare water pistol beside her hand. His eyes caught on her streaked skin. "Don't get any of the ammunition on yourself," he warned.

"Where's Aldous?" asked Rutherford, turning away from the half-melted thorn hedge.

"In the woods," Olive panted, barely able to breathe for the stinging in her legs. "But he's coming back."

"We have to get Olive out of here," said Horatio to the others. "It's been dangerously long already."

Olive tried to get to her feet, but her legs refused to hold her. She crashed back to the ground, her palms scraping the rocky earth. The water pistol slipped out of her fist and bounced away into the bracken. "I can't get up," she said through gritted teeth.

"We'll have to help her," Leopold ordered. "Harvey, put down that gun and get over here."

Rutherford and the three cats had just managed to help Olive balance on her numb feet when, from the bracken behind them, there came a snap.

The snap was followed by a deep, soft chuckle.

The three cats froze as though someone had disconnected their batteries. Olive turned around, falling to one knee. Rutherford took a startled step back.

As Aldous McMartin strode gracefully across the flowering hillside, the clouds began to thicken. Darkness poured across the landscape. Gathered around Olive, the three cats gave small, frightened jerks.

"I disposed of your painted assistants, Olive," said Aldous, stepping closer. "A piece of flint, a bit of fire." He smiled that same twisted, predatory smile, and

Olive felt her stomach plunge toward her big toe. "There are even simpler ways to get rid of *these.*"

While Olive teetered on her numb hands and knees, searching desperately for the lost water pistol, Aldous made a motion with his hand—a gesture so small that it almost didn't exist—and whispered something under his breath.

Leopold fell first. His long black body hit the ground and curled into a ball that jerked and writhed, then stretched out all four legs as though he were trying to run away from himself. He let out a howl that Olive had never heard before.

"NO!" she screamed, forgetting the lost water pistol and lunging on all fours at Aldous. But her rubbery limbs wouldn't hold her. She collapsed to the ground, much too far away to reach him. Twin jets of pain raced up her legs.

Harvey was the next to fall. His yowl joined Leopold's, which was already dying to a whimper. Rutherford watched from a few feet away, clutching his water pistols and jiggling desperately from foot to foot.

On her numb hands, Olive hauled herself across the ground. "Don't hurt them!" she begged. "Please! You can have anything! Just don't hurt them!"

Aldous's leonine face split with a smile. "But I already have everything I want," he replied. "This house is mine. Elsewhere is mine. These disobedient beasts"—he twitched his hand and Horatio fell to the earth—"*useless* as they may be—are *mine*."

"Please, stop!" Olive pleaded, dragging herself closer.

Rutherford made a move as if to jump in the way, but Aldous's eyes flicked up, seeming to freeze the boy in place. "Would you care to be next?" he asked.

Rutherford didn't answer.

Aldous looked down at the three twitching cats. "As a matter of fact . . ." he said softly, "I'm not quite sure that I *do* want them anymore. They've been far more trouble than they're worth. I can always conjure a new familiar once I've reclaimed the house." The smile twisted again, turning Aldous's face from handsome to monstrous. ". . . So I may as well dispose of these."

Olive turned toward Rutherford, gasping. No words found their way out of her open mouth. Rutherford was frowning intently, his eyes jerking from Olive to the cats to Aldous's face.

"Let me show you how to destroy a familiar, Olive," said Aldous, gliding closer to Leopold. "It's much easier than you might think." His hand made a graceful circle in the air. An instant later, another circle, this one made of strange, deep blue flames, appeared around Leopold's weakly twitching body. Leopold's fur began to smoke.

Frantically, Olive hauled herself across the brush.

Her hands were numb; so numb that she barely felt the scratches that should have drawn blood, though no blood made its way through her painted skin; so numb that she hardly noticed it when her palm hit something hard—something plastic—which was just the right size to be grasped in her fist.

"Stop," she commanded, raising the water pistol. "Or I'll shoot."

Aldous's eyes left Leopold. They fixed on Olive's hand, wrapped around the water pistol. In spite of the numbness, Olive could almost feel a pinprick of ice where his gaze landed. Aldous raised his hand, about to make the magical sign that would rip the pistol from her fist, just as Annabelle had once ripped away her flashlight. And as Aldous stepped closer, his yellowish eyes honed on Olive's fist, Rutherford finally got his chance. With both water pistols raised, he leaped over the three fallen cats and squirted Aldous McMartin directly in the face.

Aldous halted. Behind him, the circle of blue flames disappeared, and the three writhing cats fell silent. For a moment, Aldous looked vaguely surprised, as though he'd heard someone far away calling his name. He brushed at his face with one hand. Then he paused again, and the vaguely surprised look became much less vague. His eyes traveled slowly down his arm to his hand.

Where five long, bony fingers had been, nothing remained but five pale smudges. His cheek, where he had rubbed it, was now only a blurry gap, revealing a splotch of the golden forest behind him.

"What have you . . ." he whispered. But before he could finish the question, Rutherford fired again, and Aldous's words became only a gasp.

While Rutherford squirted both pistols, Horatio got unsteadily to his feet, followed a moment later by Harvey. The two cats threw themselves at Aldous, yowling, claws out, teeth bared. At last, Leopold pulled himself up onto his paws as well. With wisps of smoke still trailing from his fur, he charged into action, flying straight at Aldous's chest. His furious hiss echoed away across the hillsides.

Olive lay in the bracken, pinned to the ground by pain. Her legs sizzled. Her hands refused to grasp the water pistol; she felt it slip out of her fingers once again. Holding herself up on her elbows, she watched the battle unfold.

Aldous's streaked skin dripped. Each time he moved, his body blurred a bit more, like the tip of a melting icicle. The bracken below him grew smudged and muddy. The cats and Rutherford surrounded him, Rutherford still squirting both guns, the cats hissing and smearing and scratching at him with their paws.

Soon Aldous stopped trying to fight off his attackers. He raised his arms to protect his face, and his cuff wiped away the edge of his chin. Through the whirl of circling cats, Olive watched Aldous's features disappear. The sharp line of his jaw dissolved into his shirt collar. The reddish waves of his hair ran down his shoulders, dripping like rain onto the ground. Horatio slashed with one paw, and Aldous's yellow eyes vanished, first into a streak of paint, and then, with another paw-slash, into nothing.

Before she quite believed what she saw, all that remained of the young Aldous McMartin were a few smeared spots on the bracken, a mud-colored puddle where the dissolved paint had pooled, and a mess on each of the cats' paws.

The cats stood, spattered with paint, breathing hard, in a tight and wordless circle. They glanced at one another, and then at themselves, checking for any lasting injuries.

"Ugh," said Horatio at last. "I would like to wash myself."

"Use your tongue," said Harvey, who was busily taking his own advice.

"I am *not* going to use my tongue," said Horatio.

Rutherford, panting and posing like a victorious knight in his paint-splotched pajamas, turned around to look at Olive. The pride on his face drained swiftly away.

"Olive?" he called.

But Olive couldn't answer.

If she opened her mouth, all that would have come out was a scream. The red-hot pins and needles had traveled all the way to her shoulders. When she tried to bend her legs and get back to her feet, her knees sent shock waves of pain through the muscle and bone. She could barely keep her eyes open.

In a pin-pricked, burning blur, she saw her friends gather around her. She let out a stifled squeal as Rutherford raised her arm and wrapped it around his shoulders. Then came the funny sensation of being lifted, of having her legs hoisted and her pajama cuffs raised in someone's teeth, and of floating along just above the brambly ground, until she was sliding back out of the painted hills and into the darkness of the house.

V OICES HISSED AND murmured around her like
sounds made behind a locked door. Olive could
hear them, but they seemed far off and unimportant.
They had nothing to do with her.

"Where should we take her?" asked one voice.

"To her bedroom," whispered another. "Lift, men!"

Olive felt her heels dragging along the hallway
carpet. Rug-burn shot up her legs, mingling with the
pricks of a million red-hot pins, but she couldn't lift
her feet. She couldn't even lift her *eyelids*. Then, suddenly, she was falling backward, and something much
squishier than the bracken of the painting was catching her. Tendrils of pain spiraled through her limbs.
She squinted up through the darkness, trying to focus
on the three pairs of bright green eyes and the single
pair of smudgy lenses that floated above her.

"Maybe I should get my grandmother," Rutherford proposed.

"This isn't your grandmother's sort of magic," said Horatio.

"Should we wake her parents and take her to the hospital?"

"And explain this *how?*" Horatio demanded in a whisper. Everyone was quiet for a moment. "There is nothing a hospital can do for her," said Horatio at last. "Doctors are not trained to treat injury by magical paints."

Leopold's voice spoke up. "She's going to make it," he said firmly, although Olive could hear the hint of fear under his words. "We got her out in time."

Something warm and fuzzy pressed itself against Olive's chest.

"I hear a heartbeat," Horatio whispered. *"Olive."*

Olive blinked. Horatio's wide orange face hovered in the slit between her eyelids. "Olive, you must keep moving. You need to get the blood flowing."

Olive tried to swat Horatio away, but she couldn't even raise her hand. A zing of pain shot down her arm.

"That's it, Agent Olive!" said a voice from somewhere near Olive's feet—or where her feet had been when she last remembered feeling them. "Target practice!" Harvey urged. "Try to kick me!" His paw prodded her ankle. "Come on!"

Weakly, Olive wiggled her foot. She had learned

what frostbite felt like several years ago, while building a snow fort with bare hands, and she still remembered that burning, aching pain. Now she felt as though her whole body had been rolled in a snowbank. She sucked in a breath through her teeth.

"Is that the best you can do?" taunted Harvey.

Olive wiggled and winced again.

Harvey executed a barrel roll across her ankles. "A good agent thinks three steps ahead of the enemy," he whispered. "Come on, Agent Olive, take aim, and—"

Olive booted Harvey off the end of the bed.

A zing of pain shot upward from her toes. "Ow!" she groaned.

"Excellent shot, miss," said Leopold.

"She'll be all right," said Horatio.

Olive knew that she should feel relieved. She knew that lying in her own bed, with the painted Aldous destroyed and all of her friends surrounding her, was a pretty good place to be. But something was missing. Something . . . Olive twitched her buzzing fingers. No. *Someone.*

"Morton!" she croaked.

"What about him?" asked Rutherford.

"He's out there," Olive panted. "On his own. With the painted Horatio." Panic swelled in her chest like a growing fire as she realized just how long Morton had been out of sight, out of Elsewhere . . . "He's going to run away!" she gasped.

"What are you talking about, Olive?" asked Horatio, from close to her side.

"He's going to leave," Olive managed, "and get lost or hurt and never come back!"

"We'll find him, miss," said Leopold. "Don't worry."

"Special forces are on the case," Harvey added, leaping back onto the bed.

"Where did you see him last?" asked Rutherford.

"He was going downstairs. Following the other Horatio."

"Stay here," Horatio commanded. "Just keep moving your arms and legs. We'll take care of this."

The three cats zoomed out the door with Rutherford tiptoeing after. Olive heard their soft steps recede into the distance.

She stared up at the dark ceiling and tried twitching her fingers, one by one. They flared with little zapping burns. She stopped, feeling strangely exhausted. It was the middle of the night, after all, and she had been in and out of paintings, falling into pits, running through forests and hills and hallways. And her bed was so comfy . . .

But falling asleep was a terrible idea. Horatio had said to keep moving. And Morton and Horatio's imposter were still somewhere in the house—or somewhere outside of it.

Olive kicked her feet nervously. She turned her head from side to side, which didn't hurt too badly, and then started to lift herself up on her arms, which hurt a *lot*.

Olive dropped back on the pillows. She tried to listen to the sound of her blood moving through her body, imagining it flowing into the painted places, hissing and crackling and steaming like hot water hitting a sheet of ice. She could hear her heart beating in her ears, *thump, thump,* low and soft and steady.

Thump. Thump.

Then, from somewhere much farther away, she heard another thump.

Thump. Thump.

Olive turned her head to one side, craning toward the open bedroom door. The hallway lay beyond, glowing faintly with moonlight. It was empty.

But Olive heard it again.

Thump. Very soft. Soft, but clear.

Olive's heart began to beat a bit faster. The other thump did not speed up. And then Olive realized what the thumping was.

Someone was climbing up the stairs.

"Rutherford?" Olive called, in a whisper.

But the steps were slow, unlike Rutherford's.

Thump.

"Horatio? Leopold?"

But these steps came one at a time, unlike the cats'.

"Hello?" Olive whispered.

There was no answer.

Thump.

The step was very soft. And very close.

Biting her cheek to keep from screaming, Olive rocked onto one side. Her legs and arms roared with pain as she rolled across the bed and slipped over its edge. She hit the floor with a light *smack*. Gathering the last bit of strength in her limbs, Olive wormed her way underneath the bed and froze, barely breathing, with her eyes peeping out beneath the dust ruffle, staring at the open door.

A soft creak came from the hall. A shadow glided along the floor, just inside the open doorway.

A figure stepped into that shadow.

Olive's eyes traveled up from the hem of the long, prim skirt, to the starched shirt cuffs, to the string of pearls, to the pretty, changeless, terrifying face.

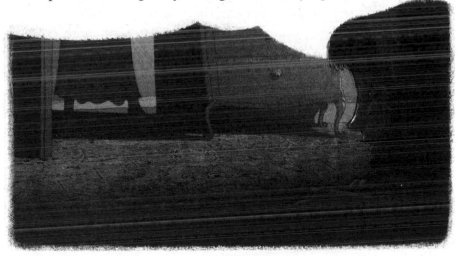

Annabelle's eyes flickered around the room. They took in Olive's vanity, with its rows of pop bottles, Olive's cluttered dresser, the twisted blankets on Olive's bed. Olive held her breath. Every other worry and plan and idea fled from her brain. All she knew was that she was playing out her own worst fears *backward*—Annabelle was the one standing in her bedroom, and *she* was the one hiding under the bed.

Annabelle's eyes skimmed the room again, resting for one long, awful second on the rumpled bed. Then Annabelle stepped out of the doorway and glided off along the hall.

Olive lay under the bed, brain clicking, heart thundering.

What should she do? Where was Annabelle going, and what was she after? Should Olive confront her on her own? And with what? Should she scream for help, waking her parents, putting them in danger too, and bringing this whole teetering tower of fragile secrets crashing down?

There were no more sounds from the hallway.

Olive squirmed forward on her prickling palms and hauled herself out from under the bed. She crawled to the doorway. Moonlight painted the hall in shades of gray, leaving deep shadows at either end. Annabelle had vanished into the darkness.

Still crawling, breathing through her teeth, Olive

dragged herself down the hallway to the bathroom. She groped along the counter for the box of matches. At least she'd have one weapon against Annabelle . . . however weak it was.

Olive climbed like a wobbly monkey up the handles of the bathroom drawers until she was standing on both feet. Her legs still felt like they were asleep, but at least the pain had lessened. Olive staggered out of the bathroom and down the dark hall to the lavender room.

The door's black mouth hung open, the antique furniture and Annabelle's empty portrait frame glittering like teeth inside. The room was empty.

Olive edged down the hall, checking each room for Annabelle, just as she'd done every day for weeks. It had been frightening even in the middle of the afternoon, with daylight streaming through the windows. She had never imagined doing it in the black of night, all alone, with her body half paralyzed, *knowing* that Annabelle was already there.

She stumbled to the door of the blue room. It was empty too. Olive slid along the wall, clutching the matches even tighter as she passed the painting of the Scottish hills, where a small blurry patch had appeared in the foreground. But as Olive glanced at the canvas, she felt a draft of cold night air thread its way through her pajamas. For a moment, she thought the wind had come from the painting, just as it had before . . . But without Aldous inside it, controlling the elements of Elsewhere, that couldn't be. No—the breeze came from the pink bedroom, through the very last doorway in the long, dark hall.

Olive lunged through the door, holding her matches ready.

Annabelle wasn't there.

The windows had been pulled wide open. Their lacy curtains rippled in the chilly breeze. Filtering through the lace, a distant streetlamp scattered its glow across the room, catching on something that had not been there before.

Standing in the center of the bedroom, its drop cloth pooled around its wooden legs, was Aldous's easel. Aldous's *empty* easel. The portrait of Aldous McMartin was gone.

"SO ALDOUS AND Annabelle are together again,"
said a voice in the darkness behind her.

Olive whirled around and almost toppled off her
feet. Rutherford stood behind her, armed with his
squirt guns.

"Rutherford!" Olive gasped. "You scared me!"

"I apologize," said Rutherford, with a little bow.
"That was not my intention."

Olive nearly smiled. In fact, she nearly said some-
thing like, *That's all right,* or *I'm so glad to see you,* or *Thanks
for coming to find me,* but she stopped herself in the nick
of time. She was still angry at Rutherford, after all—
even if it was suddenly very difficult to remember just
what she was angry *about.* She worked her face into a
frown "How did you—"

But Rutherford hurried on without meeting her eyes. "She must have heard you coming. I think she likes having the element of surprise on *her* side. She's probably taking the portrait someplace safe, reformulating her plans."

"But how did you know she was here?" Olive demanded. "How did you know about Aldous's portrait?"

Rutherford jiggled on his feet for a moment. "I'll explain later," he said. "We still haven't found Morton, or the false Horatio. We could call him The-fake-io. Or Horati-faux. Get it?"

"No," growled Olive.

"I suppose we should get back to searching," said Rutherford.

Olive wobble-stomped past him before he could confuse her any more. She was able to make it to the head of the stairs by leaning on the banister and making lots of little aggravated grunting noises. Gripping the railing tightly, she struggled down the first three steps in the time it would usually have taken her to get down the stairs, out the front door, and all the way to the edge of Linden Street. Rutherford stayed beside her, bouncing with obvious impatience.

"That's it," he urged in a whisper. "Just ten more steps to go. That's only a little more than three times as many as you've already done."

"You sound like my dad," Olive grumped, edging her toes onto the next stair.

Before she could put her rubbery foot down, there was a soft *bang* from below.

"That sounded like a door closing," said Rutherford.

Olive gave up on walking down the stairs in the usual fashion. Instead, she sat down and scooted the rest of the way on her backside, with Rutherford hustling beside her.

Harvey streaked through the foyer in front of them, skidding to a halt at the foot of the staircase. "Suspicious activity detected," he hissed into his imaginary transistor watch.

"What was that?" whispered Leopold, racing silently down the hall from the basement.

"It came from the library," Horatio murmured. The big orange cat had been watching from the shadows at the foot of the staircase, keeping so still that no one had noticed him until now.

The five of them slunk across the entryway toward the library's heavy double doors. Olive pressed her ear to the polished wooden panels. There were no sounds from the other side. Grabbing the handles and giving one quick push, Olive threw the doors open.

Moonlight fell through the library's tall, narrow windows, outlining everything in bands of soft blue.

The frame around the painting of the dancing girls glittered gently. Rows of books bound in every color were bleached to shades of silver and gray. And, in the middle of the room, on the center of the large, faded rug, sat the *other* Horatio. His silhouette glinted like metal. His painted eyes barely flickered.

Venturing into the room, Olive glanced around, confirming what she'd already feared. Morton wasn't there.

Horatio—the *real* Horatio—stepped slowly onto the edge of the rug, facing his identical enemy.

"You," he murmured. "You *monster.*"

"You," murmured the painted Horatio. "You *moron.*"

"You are the moron," snapped Horatio. "You're still held in the McMartins' thrall, blind to the pointless cruelty of everything they do."

"Don't lecture me, you traitor," the painting snapped back. "The thought that *I* have turned into *you* sickens me."

"Don't lecture *me,* you shortsighted fool." Horatio stepped forward. "In time, you would have done the same."

"I most certainly would *not.*" The painted Horatio took a step forward too.

"You most certainly *would.*" The two Horatios stood nose to nose, their identical whiskers twitching, their matching green eyes glaring at each other. It looked as though Horatio was arguing with his own reflection. The vision was so extremely odd that Rutherford, Leopold, and Harvey simply stared at it, not moving, not speaking. Even the dancing girls in the painting seemed to be watching from the corners of their eyes. Olive wavered at the edge of the room, tugged between rushing back into the darkness to search for Morton and staying to make sure that the painted cat wouldn't get away.

"In time, you would have come to see things exactly as I have," Horatio went on. "You would have seen that the McMartins were no better than the ordinary people who—"

"Yes, *ordinary*. Implying *not special*."

Horatio shook his head angrily The painted Horatio shook his too.

The real Horatio spoke next. "You serve these malignant beings not because you admire them, but because you fear them."

"*You* serve a dimwitted girl for absolutely no reason at all."

"I no longer serve anyone," growled Horatio.

"Then what is the point?" the painting growled back.

Horatio halted, struck speechless for the first time.

"What is the point of you? Of your existence?" the painted Horatio pressed on. "What is a familiar without a master? Will you simply dawdle through the millennia as a useless *housecat*?"

Horatio still did not answer.

"In fact, you are worse than a housecat. You don't even catch mice." The painting moved closer, his chilly face stopping just half an inch from Horatio's. "So tell me: *What is the point of you?*"

Silence fell over the room, as sudden and total as a blackout. No one moved. The high, dark walls seemed to lean in around them, as though the entire *house* was waiting for Horatio's answer.

"The point is, we love him," said Olive, so abruptly that she startled herself. She blinked around for a moment, wondering if the words had actually come out of her mouth or someone else's.

Both Horatios turned to stare at her. The real Horatio looked stunned. The painted Horatio looked disgusted, as though Olive had said that the point was that they used him as a toilet brush.

"They *love* you?" the painting repeated. He turned to the real Horatio, a sarcastic smirk unrolling across his face. "Awww. They *love* you. Doesn't that make eternal non-life worth living? They *love* you. They—"

Horatio lunged forward, knocking his doppelganger backward onto the rug. A split second later, the two cats had become a snarling mass of fur and claws, rolling through the patches of moonlight and disappearing into the shadows.

Harvey made as if to leap into the fray, but Leopold stopped him with a heavy black paw. "No," Leopold warned. "This is his battle."

Olive's eyes moved from the two cats to the black gap between the library doors. If Morton was still in the house, he would certainly have heard their voices by now—and yet, he hadn't appeared. He had either been waylaid by something (or *someone,* Olive thought, her mind flashing to the image of Annabelle looming in her bedroom doorway), or he was running off into the night right now, small and out of place and alone. Dragging her attention back to the brawling cats, Olive dug her fingernails into her palms until her eyes watered, as though her own pain could somehow bring the fight to an end.

Of course, it couldn't.

The battle raged on. One pounced and the other dodged, one swiped and the other rolled, their moves synchronized like an eerie dance. The only thing that separated them was that the painted Horatio remained as sleek and calm as ever, while the true Horatio's fur was beginning to look rumpled, and his sides heaved with his breath.

"Shouldn't we shoot the imposter?" asked Harvey, looking lovingly at his little holster, then glancing up at Rutherford.

"I think Leopold's right," Rutherford whispered back. "This is Horatio's duel. And although the word *duel* itself comes from an old Latin word for *war*, it has also come to imply a fight between only two combatants."

Harvey's eyes had glazed. "So no shooting, then?" he asked.

"Remember who you are," Olive could hear the painted Horatio growl as he pinned the real Horatio to the sofa cushions. "You are not here to be loved."

"I know what I am." Horatio kicked, and the painting flew backward. "I know, because I've *chosen* it." He bounded across the cushions, knocking his enemy to the floor and leaping onto the rug after him.

For the space of three of Olive's pounding heartbeats, the cats simply glared at each other, their backs arched, their tails stiff. The painted cat's eyes gleamed dully. Horatio's glittered like candles behind green glass. Then, in the same fraction of an instant, both cats slashed out with their claws. Hooked nails glinted in the moonlight, streaking across two identical faces. There were two matching hisses as both Horatios jerked backward.

On the real Horatio's face, a deep slash ran from above his eye to the bridge of his nose, releasing a flow of blood that was oily and black in the moonlight. The painted Horatio wore the very same wound, in the very same spot . . . but no blood trickled from the gash. And, as Olive, Rutherford, and the three cats stared, the cut sealed itself, leaving no trace.

The false Horatio smiled.

"Didn't you think of that?" he asked, gazing into his opponent's bloody face. "You are never going to win this fight, you poor, pathetic pet. You can't hurt me, Horatio."

The true Horatio smiled back. "I believe I'll keep trying," he said. With a sudden jump, he knocked his opponent off of his feet, and they rolled once more into the shadows.

Olive clenched her fists even harder as the cats skidded out of sight. So much time had already slipped past. Morton wasn't coming . . . and she might already be too late. But how could she leave when Horatio was locked in battle with an enemy *she* had unloosed in the first place?

"Where could Morton be?" she whispered to Rutherford. And then, below the hissing and yowling of the two Horatios, Olive caught another sound. It was a low, throaty rumble . . . and it seemed to be coming from above.

Olive's mind stopped wavering. She wheeled toward the hallway.

"What are you doing?" whispered Rutherford, grabbing her by the sleeve.

"Finding Morton!" Olive shot back over her shoulder. "Don't let the painted Horatio get away!" Dodging Rutherford's grasp, she slipped between the library doors into the thicker darkness of the hall.

The rumbling went on as Olive slipped across the foyer. She followed it through the blackness, to the foot of the stairs, where the rumbling seeming to grow louder still. Soon it seemed to be coming not just from above, but from everywhere at once, roaring straight through the ancient stone walls, echoing in the bones of the house itself. Feeling like a tiny animal in the mouth of something huge and hungry, Olive scurried up the staircase.

The upstairs hallway was deserted, and still the rushing, rumbling sound continued, overlapped once or twice by the sound of hurried footsteps. Olive edged past the dark doorway of her own bedroom, halting when she spotted a streak of white flickering on the carpet several steps ahead.

Olive inched closer. The sound rumbled on, growing even deeper and louder, until Olive stepped into the pool of light that slipped through the crack beneath the bathroom door. She yanked the door open.

Morton stood at the far end of the room, leaning over the giant claw-footed bathtub.

"Morton!" Olive gasped.

Morton gave a little jump, glancing over his shoulder. Then he turned around, twisting the taps, and the roaring sound of water rushing through ancient pipes died away.

"You *didn't* try to escape!" said Olive, sprinting across the room and grabbing Morton in a tight bear hug.

Morton made a strange face, which Olive realized was a smile half smothered by a frown, and wriggled awkwardly out of her arms. "We made a deal," he said. "And I was doing *this.*" He stepped aside, gesturing to the tub.

Following Morton's arm, Olive took her first thorough look around.

The gigantic bathtub had been filled to the lip with water—and, apparently, with bubble soap. And bath salts. And nail polish remover. And tile cleaner. And everything and anything else that Morton could find in the cabinet under the bathroom sink. The cabinet doors hung open, the floor was littered with empty bottles and jars, and mountains of greenish foam dripped softly over the tub's edges. Keeping a cautious distance from the foam, Morton glanced back and forth from the bathtub to Olive

In the dark, worried jumble of Olive's mind, somebody flicked a light switch.

She darted through the bathroom doorway, craning over the banister toward the hallway below. "Rutherford! Horatio! In here!" she whispered. A moment later, the sound of hissing and hurried footfalls traveled through the library doors and out into the foyer.

Olive leaned over the banister, beckoning wildly, as the two brawling cats and their three referees came bumping up the stairs.

"This way!" Leopold commanded. "Gentlemen, circle to the left!"

With the moving barricade of Rutherford, Harvey, and Leopold forcing them forward, the pair of Horatios tumbled through the open bathroom door, sliding across the slippery tiles. Harvey, Leopold, and Rutherford hurried after. Olive closed the door.

Surrounded, the painted Horatio backed slowly toward the center of the room.

His not-quite-bright-enough green eyes glittered. But instead of looking indignant, or angry, or even annoyed, his face looked strangely *pleased*. "It doesn't matter what you do to me, you realize," he said softly. "You're too late. She's already been here."

"What do you mean?" growled Leopold from the corner.

A smile began to form on the painting's wide orange face. "By now, she's found the master's portrait—his *finished* portrait—and taken it safely away."

For a moment, no one moved.

"It's true," Olive whispered. "I saw her. And the picture is gone."

Rutherford spoke up. "But my grandmother placed a protective charm on the house—"

The painted cat gave a sharp, dry laugh. "Who do you think invited her in?"

"It was you," Olive breathed. "Of course,"

"I was able to distract the rest of you as she made her exit, and now both she and the painting are safely hidden once again." The cat glanced proudly around at all of them. "I've done just what I was meant to do. I've served my purpose far better than the three of you have served yours. I didn't expect much of *you*, Leopold," the painting continued. "You stuffy old fool, always happy to follow orders—*anyone's* orders, apparently." Leopold inflated like a balloon about to pop, but the painting went on. "And as for you, Harvey . . ." Harvey's eyes widened. ". . . You delusional little nit, you're about as useful as a crack in a china cup."

Harvey's eyes looked as though they might fall out of their sockets. "How dare you?!" he snarled. "You traitor, you—you -double-crossing, triple-hypocrite, quadruple- traducing—"

"But *you*, Horatio," said the painted cat, ignoring Harvey's splutterings, "you and I . . . we've always prided ourselves on our intelligence. You're letting sentiment cloud your mind." He tilted his head, squinting hard into Horatio's eyes. "I hardly recognize you anymore."

Horatio squinted back at his portrait. "I only wish I *didn't* recognize you," he said softly. And then, before anyone saw it coming—least of all his painted nemesis—Horatio sprang forward, knocking the other cat off of his feet. As the two orange cats skidded across the tiles toward the bathtub, Leopold and Harvey leaped into action. They grasped the ball of writhing cats in their teeth and claws, and tossed both Horatios into the waiting water.

A massive, bubbly tidal wave swept out over the bathroom floor. Morton jumped back with a squeak, yanking the edge of his nightshirt out of the way. Leopold and Harvey darted out of the splash zone, shaking foamy water from their coats. Olive and Rutherford watched in stunned silence as the tub became a roiling, hissing, yowling fountain. Orange-tinted bathwater, confettied with flakes of orange paint, spewed out of the tub. Every now and then, a head or a paw or the tip of a dripping wet tail would appear above the bathtub's edge before disappearing into the waves once again.

After a long expanse of splashy seconds, the water in the bathtub stilled. A few final wavelets slopped over the tub's curved sides. A trail of bubbles popped, one by one, as they struck the floor. Everyone waited. And then, at last, Horatio's scarred face—looking drenched and dark and *extremely* irritated—appeared above the lip of the tub.

"Horatio!" Olive exclaimed. But before anyone else could move or speak, there was a loud slam from

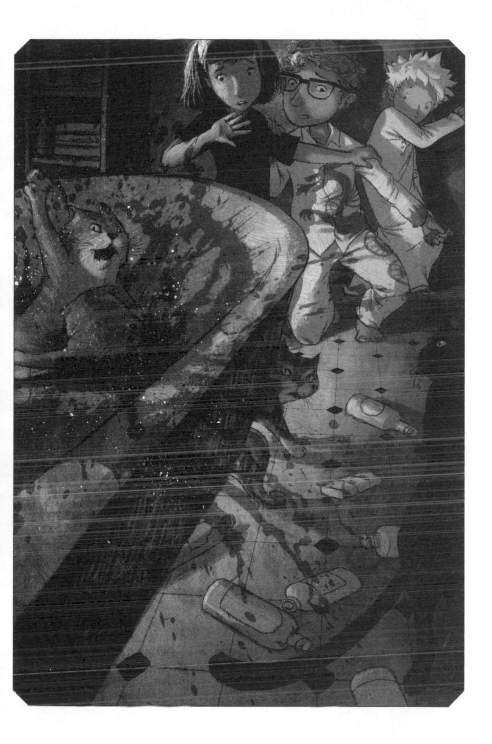

somewhere downstairs, followed by the sound of quick, heavy steps running up the staircase.

Olive's heart hit the roof of her mouth. Rutherford turned to her, a horrified expression spreading across his face. The cats froze. Morton dove behind the tub, hiding in the shadows.

The bathroom door flew open.

Mrs. Dewey stood in the doorway, panting and clutching the lapels of the flowery robe that covered her equally flowery nightgown. She glanced quickly around the flooded scene.

"She was here!" Mrs. Dewey gasped. "Annabelle! Someone must have let her in, because she didn't break the charm, which means—" Mrs. Dewey broke off as her eyes landed on her grandson. "Rutherford Dewey!" she hooted. "What on earth have you done to your pajamas?"

RUTHERFORD DIDN'T EVEN get to begin his explanation—and knowing Rutherford, it would have
been long and logical and highly detailed—before
there was the sound of yet another door creaking open.

Mr. and Mrs. Dunwoody, looking squinty and rumpled, ventured out of their bedroom at the far end of
the hall. Mrs. Dunwoody flicked on a hallway light,
which made both of them squint even more. Side
by side in their matching robes, they shuffled along
the hall, their heads craning toward the source of the
noise. At the bathroom door, they came to an abrupt
stop. Their squinting eyes widened. Their stares traveled over the two damp cats standing sheepishly in
one corner, the tub full of bubbles topped by Horatio's
annoyed face, the sopping wet floor, the neighbor boy

armed with a pair of water pistols, his panting grand-mother in her flowery nightclothes, and Olive, waver-ing nervously at the edge of the scene while clutching at her pajama pants.

"Olive . . . ?" said Mr. Dunwoody, as though he wasn't sure that he was using the right name.

"I am so sorry about all of this, Alec and Alice," Mrs. Dewey jumped in. "Rutherford has recently been prone to occasional bouts of sleepwalking—"

"Yes," interrupted Rutherford. "And sleep-trespassing. And sleep-cat-bathing."

"It's been very upsetting," said Mrs. Dewey.

"Particularly for the cats," added Rutherford.

"Oh," said Mrs. Dunwoody, blinking at the bathtub. Horatio stared back at her through slitted eyes.

"We do apologize for waking all of you," said Mrs. Dewey, glancing from Olive to her parents, "and we appreciate your understanding."

"Please don't apologize," said Mr. Dunwoody, who looked as though he was just beginning to realize that he wasn't dreaming. "I'm just glad that he sleepwalked here, someplace where he would be safe."

Rutherford and Olive exchanged a look.

"Yes," said Mrs. Dewey. "Well, after we clean up this mess, I am going to get him back home and into his own bed. Fetch a towel, Rutherford."

"No, no," said Mrs. Dunwoody. "We'll mop up. You

two go get some rest. This must have been a frightening experience for both of you."

"I'll walk them to the door," Olive announced,
before either of her parents could offer.

Olive and the Deweys thumped down the stairs.
Mrs. Dewey waited until they were out of Mr. and
Mrs. Dunwoody's earshot. Then she whispered, "As
far as I could tell, Annabelle was gone before I even
reached your door. She must have simply run in and
run back out again. I don't know what she was after,
but—"

"We know," Olive said quietly. "Rutherford can tell
you."

They paused in the foyer, just inside the heavy front
door. The moon threw long, stretched streaks of light
through the windows, like pale blue arms trying to
reach inside.

"I'll cast the charm again," Mrs. Dewey murmured.
"And Olive, I think it would be a good idea for you
to visit my house now and then—shall we say once a
week? There are a few things I could teach you." She
opened the front door and paused for a moment, carefully scanning the porch, the steps, and the front lawn.
All was quiet. With a last little smile at Olive, she
moved her round, flowery body through the door.

Olive and Rutherford hesitated at the threshold. A
draft of dewy night air swirled around them. It chilled

Olive's damp clothes, making her skin prickle, and she realized that all the numbness had gone at last.

She turned to Rutherford. In a whisper that she hoped his grandmother couldn't catch, she demanded, "How did you know?"

Rutherford blinked. "How did I know what?"

"Everything! How did you know where to find me? How did you know I needed help? How did you know to bring those water pistols? How did you get the cats to help you? *How did you know?*"

"The cat part was simple," said Rutherford evasively. "Leopold was already looking for a reason to believe in you again, so I just had to explain what had been going on." He paused. "And I think Harvey just really liked the guns."

"But how did *you* know what was going on?"

Rutherford looked at Olive for a moment. Beams of moonlight turned his glasses into two smaller, flickering moons. He swayed gently from foot to foot, as though he was deciding which direction to turn. "I'm a reader," he said at last.

"I know that," said Olive impatiently. "You're *always* reading. That's why you know weird words like *plierssaur* and *spauldrons*."

"Spaulders," Rutherford corrected. "I don't mean books. I mean . . ." He paused. "I read . . . I read people's thoughts."

Olive held very still while her mind flipped busily backward through all its Rutherford-related memories. The way he had always seemed to guess what was on her mind. The funny, studying expression that would come over his face as he looked at her sometimes. The way he always seemed to pop up out of nowhere just when things were getting interesting. Suddenly, Rutherford's unbelievable statement seemed very easy to believe.

"I should have known," Olive breathed.

Rutherford nodded. "It seemed wise to postpone telling you for as long as possible. It's a much more useful quality when it's a secret. Now you *and* my grandmother know." Rutherford glanced toward Mrs. Dewey, who was waiting for him at the edge of the porch. "It's difficult to be certain of whom to trust," he added with a little shrug. "Even if you can read people's thoughts."

"I guess so." Olive hesitated. Annabelle's words, in their swirling cursive, trailed across her mind. *It's hard to know whom to trust, isn't it?* "This was the big secret Annabelle mentioned in her note, wasn't it?"

"It seems highly likely," said Rutherford. "By spying on me and my grandmother, she could easily have figured it out."

"So—can you tell what Annabelle is thinking right now?" Olive asked with a little shiver, looking out at the empty sweep of Linden Street.

Rutherford shook his head. "She's not a person. Only a portrait. It doesn't work the same way. It's the same with the cats; I can't read their thoughts at all. It's unfortunate, really. I'd love to be able to know what Harvey is thinking."

Olive smiled. "Me too."

"I generally need to look directly into a person's eyes while I read them," Rutherford went on. "However, I can read the people to whom I'm closest even from a distance—at least, that's what I've theorized. I used to believe it only worked with my own family members, but that doesn't seem to be the case. Because the only people I can read from far away are my parents, my grandmother . . . and you," Rutherford finished. "That's how I knew you needed help tonight."

Olive glanced past Rutherford at Mrs. Dewey, who was still waiting at the edge of the porch, pretending not to be eavesdropping on their conversation.

"Why didn't you tell me about this sooner?" she asked.

"You were hiding things from me," Rutherford said simply. "The spellbook, and what you'd done with it. The paints—that you'd managed to concoct and use them. It was clear that you didn't really trust *me,* so it was rather difficult for me to trust *you.*"

Olive looked down at the floorboards, tinted blue by the moonlight.

"In the interest of full disclosure," Rutherford went on, "I've made a decision. If you will *let* me help you, and if you won't hide any more big secrets from me, I think I would prefer to stay here."

Olive looked up. "You mean—you wouldn't go to that school in Sweden?"

Rutherford shook his head. "After what happened tonight, I feel fairly certain that you will accept my assistance. The truth is . . ." He paused, readjusting his smudgy glasses. "The truth is, I would rather stay here anyway. This is the first school I've attended where someone has willingly sat with me at lunch for multiple consecutive days."

Olive smiled. "Good. Then . . . yes. I'd *like* your help."

Rutherford smiled back. Then he raised one hand, turning out the palm in oath-taking position. "I, Rutherford Dewey, do hereby swear upon the honor of my family name that I—"

"No oaths," Olive interrupted. "We'll just tell the truth."

Rutherford bowed. Then he strode across the porch to join his grandmother.

"Good night, Olive," said Mrs. Dewey, guiding her grandson down the porch steps.

"Good night," Olive answered. Then she stepped inside, closed the heavy front door, and locked it firmly behind her.

Upstairs, in the bathroom, Mr. and Mrs. Dunwoody had finished sopping up the flooded floor. Olive caught the sound of their voices as she climbed the steps.

"If you sneak up behind him, dear, he'll have a very narrow angle of escape in this direction," Mr. Dunwoody was saying as Olive rounded the corner. There was a hiss, the squeal of wet feet on tile, and Horatio bounded through the door smack into Olive's shins.

Mr. and Mrs. Dunwoody, both holding large towels, peered through the doorway.

"Don't worry about the cat," said Olive as Horatio blockaded himself behind her legs. "I'll dry him off."

Mr. Dunwoody gave a relieved sigh. Mrs. Dunwoody sneezed.

"After that, will you get straight to bed?" prompted Mr. Dunwoody.

Olive nodded.

Mr. and Mrs. Dunwoody both gave her quick kisses on top of her head. Then they drifted drowsily back down the hall to their bedroom. The door clicked shut behind them.

Olive and Horatio darted back into the bathroom. Harvey and Leopold, who had been hiding behind the open door, edged back out onto the tiles. A voice behind the bathtub squeaked, "Can I come out now?" A moment later, Morton's tufty white head appeared above the tub's lip.

"We'll escort Morton home, miss," said Leopold.

"Morton," said Olive as Morton clambered out from behind the tub and straightened his nightshirt. "You saved the day."

"I know," said Morton, with a shrug of muffled pride. "I just thought, 'What cleans up paint?' and then I thought, 'Well, I might as well try everything at once.' And it worked."

"Yes." Olive looked down into the tub. A few orange-tinted bubbles still clung to the drain. "I was sure you would run away," she said. "You had the perfect chance."

Morton's round, pale face went from pleased to cagey. "You've still got two and a half months," he said.

Olive let out a deep breath. "Good." She sat down on the edge of the bathtub and popped one orange bubble with her fingertip. "But if nothing ever changes in Elsewhere, how do you know how much time has gone by?"

Morton's eyebrows went up. "I watch you," he said simply. "When it's nighttime, you go into your bedroom, and your mother or father goes in to say good night." Morton's voice grew softer. "Sometimes they stay a little bit longer, and I know they're probably tucking you in. Then you come out again, and it turns light, and it's another day. I've been counting the days in my head," he said with a faint smile. "That's how I know time is going by. That, and you look different already."

"I do?" said Olive, feeling strangely pleased. "How do I look now?"

Morton looked at Olive for a long, quiet moment. "Different," he said.

"We should be going, miss," Leopold interjected. "Duty calls."

"Surveillance will resume once Agent M is returned to his base of operations," added Harvey.

"Right." Olive got up from the edge of the tub. The last of the orange bubbles had disappeared down the drain. "Thanks, Leopold. Thanks, Agent 1-800." The cats gave satisfied nods before heading toward the door. "And thank you, Morton."

Morton smiled back. Then he followed Harvey and Leopold away into the darkness of the hall. Horatio bumped the door shut behind them.

Olive knelt on the floor and unfolded the biggest, fluffiest towel, holding it out enticingly. Horatio sighed. Then, with considerable foot-dragging and huffing, he moved closer to let Olive rub him dry.

"Does your cut hurt?" Olive asked.

"Yes," said a muffled voice from inside the towel. "But I believe it has been thoroughly sterilized."

Through the cloth, Olive rubbed his head very gently.

"It appears that Annabelle got what she came for," said the muffled voice.

A feeling of dread crushed Olive's happy mood like a cannonball dropped onto a birthday cake. "Yeah," she mumbled.

Inside of the towel, Horatio was quiet for a moment. "She might have the portrait," he said at last, "but she can't get Aldous out of it. Not without the spectacles. Or one of us."

"So . . . we're safe for now?"

"Not quite," said Horatio, stepping out of the towel and giving his fur a quick shake. "I would say that we are in danger, but the danger is not immediate."

In watchful silence, Olive, slightly damp, and Horatio, almost dry, slipped down the hall to Olive's bedroom. Hershel waited on the pillows. Olive wriggled under the covers beside him. Horatio stood just inside the doorway, watching over her until Olive settled down beneath the blankets.

"We will be patrolling the house," he said softly. "Try to get some sleep." He stepped through the door.

"Horatio," Olive called.

The cat paused. A beam of moonlight falling through the door silvered the edges of his fur.

"I hope you"—Olive struggled—"I mean, I hope—I hope you don't feel like you have no purpose. Like the other Horatio said. Because . . . I really need you."

"Yes," said Horatio with a little sigh. "Whatever would you do without me to clean up your messes, Olive?"

"No, I mean—well, yes, I've needed you to fix things I've messed up, but also—what I said before." Olive took a deep breath. "We love you. Morton, and Harvey, and Leopold . . . and me. We do."

Horatio stood still. Even the tips of his ears and the ends of his whiskers, illuminated with moonlight, didn't move. "Yes. Well," he said at last. "That's enough of a purpose for anyone."

Then he slipped through the doorway and disappeared.

"S o," said Ms. Teedlebaum, "after I found out that it wasn't a tumor, just an ingrown toenail, my life changed dramatically once again. I mean, you learn not to take things for granted—toenails especially. You should all take off your shoes and socks and just *study* your feet sometime. It really puts things in perspective."

Ms. Teedlebaum glanced around at her students, who had been listening to a twenty-two-minute history of her health issues (Olive knew this because she was watching the clock and drawing little squiggles in her notebook for each minute that went by), and heaved a satisfied sigh.

"All right," she began. "I suppose we should get focused. Now, where did I put my calendar?" Ms.

Teedlebaum stared down at the cluttered tabletop in front of her as though she had never seen it before. She flipped through several leaning towers of folders, knocked over a shoebox full of plastic lids, and looked underneath a blobby object that was probably supposed to be a papier-mâché person but that looked more like a papier-mâché zucchini. "Never mind," she announced, raising her arms. "I remember what we were doing. You were displaying your family portraits. On Monday, we'll start a new unit. Without my calendar, I can't say for certain what you will need, but please come prepared. Why don't you—" Ms. Teedlebaum broke off, grabbed the little notebook that hung around her neck, and scribbled something down. "Chopped broccoli. That was it." She glanced up again. "Get your materials and display your work. Once I've checked you off my list, you can take your portraits home to keep."

Stools squeaked as students climbed down and raced across the art room to the storage cabinets. As usual, Olive waited until everyone else was out of the way before crossing to the shelf that held her portrait of Morton's parents. But as she pulled the canvas out of its spot, something else fluttered down from the edge of Olive's shelf.

It landed on the dusty tiles near the toe of her shoe. Olive picked it up. It was a small, folded card, made of thick ivory paper. The outside was blank. On the inside, however, was a note written in fine, lady-like cursive. Olive's arms began to tremble. Staring at that familiar handwriting, she wondered for a second if she had hit a snag in the progression of time—if she had somehow skipped backward to another awful afternoon, when she had stood right here in the art room, reading her own name written by Annabelle's hand.

But *this* note didn't have her name in it anywhere.

Dear Florence, it read,

I have received your bottle cap collage and the necklace you so inventively made of acorns, buttons, and fishing lures (which I see were put to good use before being turned into jewelry, as they are all endowed with a particularly fishy smell), but I must tell you that these gifts—and your repeated thanks—are perfectly unnecessary.

In spite of your charming self-invitations, I am afraid that I do not allow visitors inside my home. The upkeep of a house of this size is simply beyond the strength of someone my age, and I wouldn't want strangers, however oblivious or persistent they may be, to see the house when it was not at its very best.

There is no need for further thanks on your part. And please— no more gifts.

Yours sincerely,

A. McMartin

Before Olive could begin to put these new pieces into the puzzle or stop her hands from shaking, a jingling sound came from over her shoulder.

"*That's* where I put it," said Ms. Teedlebaum, tugging the note out of Olive's hand. "I must have left it there to remind me. Thank you, Florence!" She gave herself a pat on the head. "I thought you might be interested in it, Olive, as this came from your house's former owner. And I've been meaning to tell you about how I met Ms. McMartin."

A throng of goose bumps skittered up the backs of Olive's arms. Even if Ms. Teedlebaum didn't have anything to do with the portrait in her attic, it would be a while before the sound of several clinking keys didn't make her skin crawl.

"I only met her once," Ms. Teedlebaum said, tugging absently at a necklace threaded with multiple whistles. "She hardly ever left the house, so I went to Linden Street to thank her in person for her *sizable* donation to the local art museum—I'm on the committee for community outreach and acquisitions—but she didn't even invite me inside the front door. And I would really have liked to look around, to see the collection of Aldous McMartin's work. I didn't get the chance to do *that* until the other day, when your mother was nice enough to let me in." Ms. Teedlebaum smiled. "But Ms. McMartin was already a very old woman at the time, and she seemed uncomfortable with being thanked, let alone having a visitor come inside her house. That's why I decided to send the thank-you gifts instead. Art speaks louder than words."

Olive managed to squeeze the words "What did Ms. McMartin donate?" past her rapidly beating heart. Were there other branches of Elsewhere—other trapped *people*—in another building, right in her own town?

"Money," said Ms. Teedlebaum. "I don't remember the exact amount, but there were a lot of zeros on that check. And a few paintings; nothing by Aldous McMartin himself, just a few pieces from the family collection."

Olive's heart tobogganed back to its usual spot.

Ms. Teedlebaum gave a little sigh. "I envy you, honestly," she said. "How inspiring, to live in a place like that."

"Um-hmm," said Olive.

"In fact, you can keep the note," said Ms. Teedlebaum, thrusting the card back into Olive's hand. "It can remind you of your house's history." Ms. Teedlebaum beamed, clearly assuming that it was gratitude that had rendered Olive completely speechless. "You're welcome," she said. "Now, as long as we're both standing here, why don't I check you off my list right now? May I see your portrait?"

Slowly, Olive held up her painting of Morton's parents.

In this second, non-magical version, she had worked hard to make their clothing look real, including all the wrinkles and rumples and folds of real fabric. Their eyes were still a bit too large, but at least they didn't look like lemurs in human suits this time. Mr. Nivens's fingers weren't quite so sausagey, and there was something in Mrs. Nivens's smile that made it look welcoming and warm and playful all at once, and this made her whole face seem almost alive.

"You paid close attention to detail, and you were careful to keep everything in scale." Ms. Teedlebaum nodded to herself. A thousand kinks of dark red hair nodded in agreement. "Beautiful job on the facial expressions. You have a real talent for this. This is something special."

Olive ducked her head and smiled.

Ms. Teedlebaum tapped her uncapped pen thoughtfully against her chin, leaving a cluster of inky freckles. "You know, Olive," she began, "if you would be willing, I'd like to keep your portrait to use as an example for future art classes. And of course it would be displayed in the Case of Fame too." Ms. Teedlebaum gestured to the glass-fronted shelves lining one wall of the room. Olive spotted several colorful canvases, some coil pots that looked as though they could have suffocated jungle mammals, and a handful of other papier-mâché people/zucchinis.

"Thank you very much," she said, "but it's a present for someone."

"Ah. I see." Ms. Teedlebaum nodded, moving away toward the table where the other students were waiting. "Well, as they say, there's no time like a present."

Still smiling to herself, Olive shuffled toward the display table. She took the stand at the very end of the row and balanced her painting of Mr. and Mrs. Nivens on it. As the rest of the class shoved and laughed and looked at each other's work, she stared into Mr. and Mrs. Nivens's painted eyes.

Where are you, Mary and Harold Nivens? she asked the painted people. *I've looked everywhere in the house, over and over. Where could you be?*

"Is that one yours?" said a voice over Olive's shoulder.

Olive jumped. She turned away from Mrs. Nivens's painted eyes to a pair of living eyes, surrounded by the thick black paint of eyeliner.

"Um . . . yes. It's mine," she mumbled.

The dark-haired girl leaned toward the canvas. "Those clothes are really weird and old-fashioned. It must have taken you forever to paint all those buttons."

"It—it took a long time."

"Are they your ancestors or something?" The girl's eyes swiveled up to Olive's again.

"Um . . ." Olive stalled. "They're sort of . . . in my extended family."

The girl nodded. "It's really good," she said, after a silent moment. Then she wandered back to her own noisy friends, leaving Olive to smile at her silent ones.

With a large, rectangular, paper-wrapped package under her arm, Olive hurried up Linden Street at Rutherford's side.

"Can you hear what everyone is thinking all the time, like a bunch of TVs all playing at once?" Olive asked. This was her eighteenth question in a row (not that Olive was keeping track), but Rutherford didn't seem to be losing patience. Rather, he appeared to be relishing the fact that someone *wanted* to hear his answers.

"No," he said. "If I heard billions of thoughts all at once, I probably couldn't understand anything at all." He gave a little bounce, shifting his giant backpack. "I have to concentrate on one person at a time, and it has to be someone I know—otherwise, how would I know whose thoughts I was hearing? In other words, I can't just decide to listen to the president's thoughts, whether or not that would be potentially criminal of me."

"Is it actually like *reading*? Or is it like hearing something?"

"It's more like dreaming, really," said Rutherford, dropping his voice as they passed Mr. Butler, at work on his hedges. Mr. Butler's eyes followed them suspiciously. "I see and hear several things at once, and not everything makes sense, and events frequently jump out of sequence. Often it looks like someone has smeared a bunch of pictures together."

"Do you think you could teach me how to do it?"

Rutherford shook his head. "My grandmother says it's something you have to be born with. It runs in families, like dimples, or being able to roll your tongue. Or curly hair." Rutherford tugged on the messy tuft above his ear. "It's fairly prevalent in magical families. Apparently, there have been other readers on our family tree, but the trait has skipped the last couple of generations."

Olive looked down at her shoes scuffing through the piles of fallen leaves and thought about how her family's math gene had skipped her particular generation.

Rutherford watched her. He nodded at the package under her arm. "I think your artistic talents more than outweigh your lack of mathematic skills."

Olive glanced up. "It's kind of weird knowing that you can look into my brain anytime, whether or not I want you to. No wonder Harvey said you were a spy. You sort of *are*."

"I promise not to do it often," said Rutherford. "I give you my word of honor. I'll even take an oath."

"That's okay," said Olive as they reached the edge of Mrs. Dewey's yard. "Just don't do it unless there's an emergency or something."

Rutherford gave her a sweeping bow. This made his giant backpack slide off his shoulder and whack him in the side, nearly knocking him off his feet. He tried to regain his dignity. "I shall read your mind only in emergency situations," he announced, holding up one palm. "Or when I *think* there is an emergency. Or when I know there's *going* to be an emergency. Or—"

"Good enough," said Olive.

"But your question reminds me," said Rutherford, beginning to jiggle excitedly from foot to foot, "you're invited to come over tomorrow afternoon. My grandmother will teach us the rudiments of protective charms and the herbs involved in their concoction. It should be very helpful, considering your situation."

Olive sighed. "I'm trying *not* to consider my situation." She glanced up the street at the towering stone house. "But I'd better go. I want to give Morton his present."

Rutherford gave Olive a sweeping farewell bow, and Olive, after bowing awkwardly back, ran up the sidewalk to the big stone house and pulled open the heavy front door.

The foyer was silent and empty. Quietly, Olive locked the front door behind her and lowered her book bag and the rectangular package to the floor. She glanced through the open doorways to either side: the dusty, double-doored, high-ceilinged library to her left, the formal parlor to her right.

Annabelle McMartin—the real, living-and-dying Annabelle McMartin—had stood in this spot not long ago, closing the door in Ms. Teedlebaum's face and locking out the world. And just yesterday, the un-living, undying Annabelle had stood here again, looking for a way to take it all back. This thought made Annabelle seem near enough that Olive could almost feel her chilly presence over her shoulder, her cold, smooth hand reaching out to lock around the spectacles and —

"Olive?"

Olive's heart executed a leap so high it bumped into Olive's molars. She let out a squeak.

Mrs. Dunwoody's smiling face appeared at the end of the hallway. "I came home early today," she announced. "I figured you could use some pampering, after another long day of junior high." Mrs. Dunwoody held up a plate. "I fixed you a snack. Celery sticks with peanut butter and raisins."

"Is it creamy peanut butter?"

"Naturally," said Mrs. Dunwoody as Olive trailed down the hall to join her in the kitchen. "I don't like the crunchy kind myself. That sort of randomness of texture distracts me."

"Thanks, Mom," said Olive, taking the plate and noticing that there were exactly six neatly aligned raisins on each celery stick.

"There's fresh orange juice in the fridge," Mrs. Dunwoody added, leafing through a stack of bills and catalogs on the counter.

"I'm going to take my snack up to my room," said Olive. "I've got some homework I want to get over with."

"We could do something fun after that, if you'd like," said Mrs. Dunwoody. "We could go to the library or rent a movie."

"Sure."

Leaving her mother humming happily over the bills, Olive hurried back down the hall, grabbed her backpack and the rectangular package, and thudded up the stairs.

But before she could open the door to her bedroom, something made her stop in her tracks.

"Ladies and gentlemen!" announced a voice from the end of the hall. "You are about to be awestruck by the feats of the greatest escape artist who has ever lived! No trickery! No fakery! Only pure superhuman skill! The one—the only—*Hairy Houdini!*"

There was a flapping, flopping sort of sound as Harvey's head appeared through the doorway to the pink bedroom. His head was gradually followed by the rest of his body, which was swaddled in bands of torn cloth, rusty chains, tasseled curtain cords, and anything else wrap-able that could be found in the attic. Harvey wormed his way down the hall toward Olive. His front legs were bound to his body, so he had to push himself along with his back feet while his head coasted like a ship's prow across the floor. Olive could hear the crackle of fur-on-carpet static from several feet away.

"Prepare to be amazed!" Harvey grunted, before flopping over onto his back and kicking wildly at his restraints. "Just a few more seconds—just—a few— more—"

Ropes and chains looped around Harvey's thrashing legs like the yarn in a game of cat's cradle. Eventually he managed to free one paw, but this quickly got stuck again in the wads of fabric.

"Mr. Houdini?" Olive asked, setting down the plate and book bag and dropping onto her knees next to the squirming cat.

"Call me Hairy," Harvey panted.

"Hairy," Olive repeated. She tried to slip a knot off

of one of Harvey's claws and got an electric shock in exchange. "Did you see any sign of the McMartins today?"

"No," Harvey grunted, finally succeeding in shaking his head out of one particularly thick loop of curtain cords. "All is calm, all is bright, as Shakespeare said."

"I don't think that was Shakespeare." Olive watched Harvey struggle for a moment. "Do you want me to help you out?"

"No need for that!" said the cat. "Three—two . . . I mean . . . Ten—nine—"

On his third attempt, Harvey managed to rock onto his side and balance on one foreleg and one hind leg. Bands of rope and chain still encircled the rest of his body, as though he had been very sloppily mummified.

"Ta-da," he declared.

Olive applauded before getting up and heading toward her bedroom. Behind her, she could hear the flop of Harvey falling over.

Horatio was seated at the foot of her bed, staring out the window, his soft, warm fur made half transparent by the afternoon sunlight. Olive set down the plate of snacks on her bedside table and tossed her book bag onto the bed. The mattress bounced. Horatio didn't move.

"Hi, Horatio," said Olive. "I'm going to take a present to Morton. It's a picture of his parents. Made with

normal paint this
time," she added
quickly. "Would you
like to come Else-
where with me?"

Horatio didn't
answer. His ears
gave a miniscule
twitch.

"Horatio?"

Slowly, Horatio's
face turned toward
Olive. "She's out
there. Not far
away."

Olive clutched
her painting to
her chest. "What
should we do?" she
whispered.

"What *can* we
do?" Horatio's
whiskery eyebrows
rose. "Be on our
guard. Keep our
eyes open. Trust
each other."

The sick sensation filling Olive's body lightened just the teensiest bit. She nodded.

"Shh," Horatio hissed suddenly.

"What?"

"Can't you hear it?"

Olive listened. From somewhere down the hall, there came a crash, followed by a string of angry muttering. "I think Harvey's still stuck in his restraints."

"Not that." Horatio's eyes fixed on the window, where the ash tree's nearly bare branches tapped softly against the glass.

Olive stared at the window through the twin tufts of Horatio's ears. She listened. She waited. But whatever Horatio was sensing, Olive didn't feel it. What she felt was the sensation of balancing on something very high and very narrow. Whether she moved backward into safety or forward into the unknown, she knew that she couldn't stay still for long.

"What is it?" she whispered to Horatio.

A tiny smile appeared on Horatio's face. "We may not have to fight alone," he said.

About the author

JACQUELINE WEST is obsessed with stories where magic intersects with everyday life—from talking cats, to enchanted eyewear, to paintings as portals to other worlds. An award-winning poet, former teacher, and occasional musician, Jacqueline now lives with her husband in Red Wing, Minnesota. There she dreams of dusty libraries, secret passageways, and many more adventures for Olive, Morton, and Rutherford.

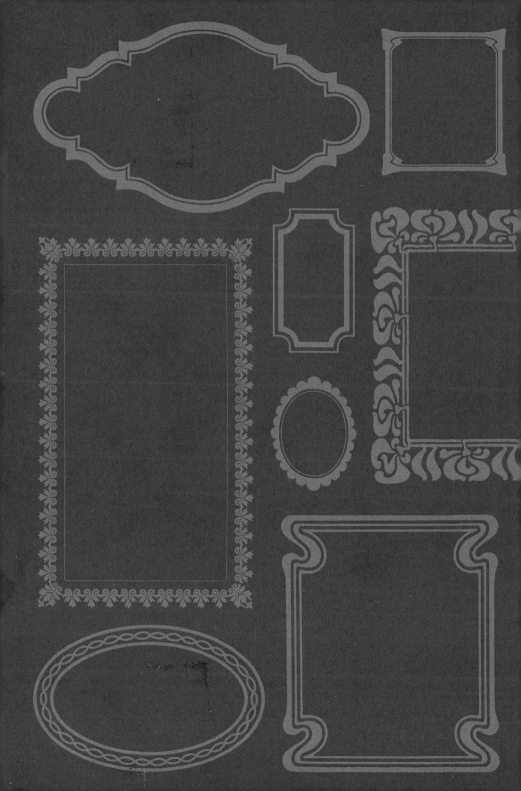